TENTACLE TRAPPED

Guardian Mates: Book Two

By Lyra Lorne

Contents

To all the monster fuckers looking for tentacles

Come on in, the water's fine.

CONTENT WARNING

Tentacle Trapped takes place in a fantasy setting, but it takes place in a world that has some darker themes. Please take care of your mental health and read over my list of trigger warnings before reading this book. You can find a full list of trigger warnings for Tentacle Trapped at www.lyralorne.com.

PRONUNCIATION GUIDE

When I started writing this book, I had an ingenious idea. I wanted my monster tentacle dude to have a Lovecraftian/Cthulhu – esque name in homage to the big tentacle daddy himself, Cthulhu. I clearly did not think about what that would be like when I had to repeatedly remember how to spell it. While writing this book, there was a lot of "Ah fuck—it's Octo—uh—what was the next letter—eh screw it." *copies and pastes name*

Then I realized I had to keep the theme going for ALL the side characters, and I ended up with a lot of names that I couldn't readily spell or actually pronounce. I was committed to this vision though, and I really do like the names.

If you're anything like me, when you're reading a book with a long, complicated Fae name, it ends up becoming just a random jumble of sounds in your head. So, here's a quick little pronunciation guide for the characters in this story.

- Naomi - na-OH-mee

- Cindy - SIN-dee

- Nathan - NAY-thuhn

- Octhogh'xu - oc-THO-gh-SHOO (aka Octo aka

that fucking octopus)

- Xaiolpa - sigh-OL-pa

- Ovaggd'tho - O-vahg-d-THO

- Cthegril - KUH-THUH-grill

- Vrala - v-RALL-a

- Ziopi – ZEE-oh-PEE

To any linguists that may be reading this, I am truly sorry for the horror that I probably just inflicted on you.

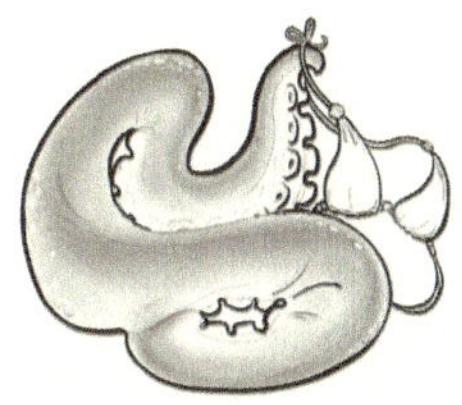

Chapter 1

Naomi

Last night—after several flight delays—I arrived at the island where my best friend is having her destination wedding.

Flying has never been my thing, and I always end up with a lot of anxiety when I travel.

Unfortunately, I hit the airport bar a little too hard during my last layover. Then when I arrived at the resort, Cindy greeted me with a drink in hand, ready to celebrate. She'd already planned a lavish dinner and drinks that night for the wedding party.

It was a lot of fun *last night*. *This morning*, not so much. I woke up early and have the hangover from hell, and I already know that Cindy will want to get drinks with the girls tonight since her wedding is tomorrow.

My head is pounding and I feel like I might throw up, so I decide that I need to take the morning to relax and recover. I grab a couple of pain killers and chug a glass of water, hoping that it helps. Then I look out the patio windows and decide to go for a walk on the beach.

If I'm going to feel like shit, I might as well do it on a beautiful beach. I can swim a little and then nap on a towel and drink lots of water. Lots and lots of water.

I change into my swimsuit and throw a sheer coverup over it. I don't bother to look in the mirror to see how I look. I've always been the "fat" friend, and feeling comfortable with how I look in a swimsuit is hard enough when I don't feel like shit. I fill up the largest water bottle I can find with water and grab a clean towel. Then I toss those and a few other items that I'll need in a large tote bag.

The walk to the beach was a little more brutal than I would like to admit. At first, the sun was so bright that I could barely open my eyes. I had tears streaming down my cheeks even with sunglasses on. Thank the gods no one was out here to see that. Somehow, I manage to make it down the walkway to the beach.

It was worth it though because the beach is so peaceful and quiet. The sky is clear and it's a beautiful day.

I head straight to the water and splash my feet in. Nothing feels better than dipping your feet in the ocean. I take a moment to dig my toes into the cool, wet sand.

I sigh and look at the horizon. It's so beautiful here. Shimmering sand and sparkling blue waters surrounded by lush, green tropical plants, bright flowers, and tall palm trees. There are even exotic birds perched in the trees. Cindy couldn't have chosen a better place for her wedding.

A tiny bubble of sadness surfaces inside me. Cindy has been my best friend forever; we've always been inseparable. Once she's married, where does that leave me? How are things going to change between us? What about whenever she has kids? I'm not married, and not even dating anyone, and I'm terrified that we are going to drift apart because of it. A lot of the other women in the wedding party are already married or engaged. I'm the only single one and it's beginning to make me self-conscious.

As I feel the fear beginning to take hold, I do what my therapist told me to do. I close my eyes, take a deep breath, and hold it for four seconds. Then I exhale for four seconds. I repeat that another time, and it seems to calm me down. I remind myself that nothing will change between Cindy and me. We will still be best friends. I'm only afraid because of my parents and the way they were.

I'm not unwanted now. I take another deep breath to help clear my head, then I focus on the sounds around me.

When I open my eyes, I feel better. Well, not physically better...but emotionally better. Physically, I still have the hangover from hell.

Cindy told me that there's an alcove just down the beach and I decide to check it out. A nice private place where I can lay out and be lazy sounds amazing.

I pop my earbuds in and start walking through the shallow water in the direction that she showed me.

As I walk, movement out in the water catches my eye. I stop and watch the waves. I could have sworn I saw something. Maybe it was a dolphin?

I keep walking, but I can't shake that nagging feeling that I'm being watched. I look around, but don't see anyone; maybe I'm just imagining it all.

My head is still pounding, so I decide to just ignore that feeling and keep walking. As I walk, I find a couple of really large and interesting shells that have washed up on the beach. I carefully pick them up and make sure they don't have inhabitants. Once I'm certain that they are empty, I put them in my bag.

I can see the wall of the alcove ahead, but it's not nearly as close as I want it to be. I'm seriously dragging right now.

I'm sweating and my legs feel like they're filled with lead. Maybe a walk wasn't a great idea with a hangover.

Cindy said there is a little cave-like entrance that takes you through a short tunnel into the alcove, so when I finally get to the wall, I start looking for it.

I find the cave entrance pretty quickly and go through the tunnel. When I reach the other side, I'm stunned by how beautiful it is. I just stand there for a minute looking around. This was definitely worth the uncomfortable walk here.

The sand is golden and smooth with no one to disturb it. The walls are dark and rocky with patches of tall green grasses growing on the tops of them. Intermixed in the green grass are spots of bright colorful flowers. Some of the flowers are growing on vines that hang over the walls of the alcove. The water is a perfect blue and is nearly as smooth as glass. It's truly breathtaking.

I set my stuff in the sand near the water and take off my cover up. I stuff it in my bag and get out the sunscreen.

As I'm applying sunscreen, I get that nagging feeling again that I'm being watched. I look around me, but there's no one else here. They couldn't even be hiding anywhere. I try to shake off the feeling again. Maybe it's just that I'm hungover.

I wipe sweat from my forehead; I have to tell Cindy I can't drink like that again tonight. I take a big gulp from my water bottle for good measure, then walk out into the water.

The water is so calm here. Due to the way the walls enclose this small beach with the rocks going pretty far out into the water, there aren't any waves. I sit down in the water and submerge myself to my chest, then lay back for a moment to put my hair in the water. It feels so good against my hot skin and my headache lessens a bit.

A splash sounds somewhere nearby and I sit up to look around, but I still don't see anything. It's the ocean, fish are going to splash sometimes, so I try not to worry about it too much. I sit in the water for a little bit longer enjoying the coolness against my skin.

Just as I'm about to stand up, I hear a much larger splash. This one sounded closer than the other one. I stand up and look around, but I don't see any big shadows in the water or anything strange. The water isn't even that deep; certainly I would see something like a shark easily.

It spooks me a little though, so I decide to go relax on the sand. I brought a book that I've been excited to read, and this is the perfect place to do some reading.

Once I get out, I spread out my towel and lay down on my stomach so I can read. As I'm lying there reading, a tiny sand crab comes scurrying by my book and stops to inspect it for a second, then scurries off again. The cute little guy makes me smile.

I have my back to the ocean as I'm reading, so I don't see anything when I hear another splash. I roll over to look, but I still can't see anything. Something feels really off about this, though. I tell myself that whatever it is, it's in the water so I don't need to worry about it and go back to reading.

At some point I must have fallen asleep, because I suddenly jolt awake from a nap. It was one of those deep naps where you wake up not even knowing your name. I look around bewildered.

I'm just beginning to get my bearings when I realize a large shadow is cast over me. Before I can even react, something wraps around my right ankle, and I'm yanked off my towel toward the ocean. I scream, then roll over to try to grab at whatever has my ankle. I scream even louder when I see what it is.

A large, thick, purple tentacle is wrapped around my leg. It's wrapped all the way up to my knee. But this tentacle isn't attached to an octopus; it's attached to a monster.

A monster that has a huge, hulking form with broad shoulders and thick, muscular arms. His whole body is mottled in purples and blues. His torso is thick and muscular, and smooth except some very large scars. He's massively strong. The lower half of his body is a mass of thick tentacles.

His head is shaped like an octopus with a bulging mantle coming off the back giving the appearance of hair. One side of his face is scarred and he's missing an eye, so he only has one golden octopus eye, two slits for a nose on his muzzle, and a mouth fringed by a beard of tentacles. I catch a glimpse of sharp teeth in his mouth.

As I take all of this in, I scream again and start kicking him with my free leg. This only serves to make him wrap another thick tentacle around my other leg. He drags me toward the water, and I claw deep gouges in the sand, trying to get away.

As soon as we reach the water, he lifts me into his massive arms and holds me tightly against his chest. His strength is crushing, and it's hard to catch my breath, but I still try to wiggle and thrash.

With all the fighting I'm doing, I only just now realize how deep the water is getting. It's up to my waist while he's holding me.

He's dragging me out to sea!

Oh gods, he's going to drown me!

I thrash and fight as hard as I can. This just makes his arms band more tightly around me.

I'm facing his body, so in desperation I lean in and bite him as hard as I can on that spot where his neck connects to his shoulder. He makes a garbled yelling sound, then growls. I can taste the metallic tang of his blood in my mouth, and blue blood runs from his shoulder.

In the next second, we dive into the water as he launches us away from the beach.

Oh gods, I can't breathe. I was screaming when he dove, and I didn't get a breath in. My lungs already feel tight and I can feel my pulse pounding in my ears.

I continue to thrash against him.

My lungs are burning. They feel like they're on fire. Blackness is beginning to creep into the edges of my vision, and it sounds like my heartbeat is thundering in my ears. I try to thrash against him again, but I'm getting weaker.

He finally stops and studies me with that one ominous eye. I see the flash of his teeth a second before he buries them into the side of my neck. The pain is instant and searing. I can feel the suction as he drinks blood from me.

I open my mouth to scream, but my body tries to suck in air instead and gets nothing but water. I thrash for a moment longer, then I finally feel my muscles go limp as my vision fades to black.

Chapter 2

Octhogh'xu

This female is mine.

While patrolling my beaches, I caught a taste of her scent and knew that she was meant for me. It surprised me when I followed her scent and saw that she's a human, but I'm not one to question these things. Her scent calls to me, so she is my mate. She's a gift from the Gods of the Sea. This time I know—this one is meant for me, and I will hunt her and claim her the way I should.

From the water, I watched her walk along the beach. I watched with curiosity as she picked up two shells and put them in the bag she carries. I don't understand why she would want the cast-off shells of dead sea creatures, but I have never understood the ways of humans.

I watched her go to the small beach and settle in, dropping her defenses. Once she was settled, I knew I just had to wait for the right moment. I was so intrigued by her that I continued to move toward her finding different places to watch her from; I was afraid she discovered me a few times. But when she fell asleep, I knew that my moment had arrived.

As quickly and quietly as possible, I charged toward her and grabbed her. She fought me well, and I'm glad of that—it shows that she's strong and hardy. Any good female mate would fight her male at first to make sure he's worthy of her. I was shocked when she bit me. It could only mean that she was so eager to mate me that she couldn't wait for me to bite her.

I gave her my mating bite, but I fear that it was not soon enough. In my eagerness to claim my mate, I did not think about her needing air. I watched as her body went limp and her chest stopped moving. I feared that I have already lost her, but then I saw the slits of the gills form on both sides of her throat. They opened and fluttered, and her whole body spasmed as she took her first underwater breath.

She's still not awake, but that is just as well. Her body is going through changes to live underwater with me, and she does not need to be awake for that. I look at her hands and am pleased to see that webbing has grown between her fingers. I glance at her feet, and her toes have elongated to about twice their original length. They have grown webbing between them as well.

Good, good. This is all well and right.

Her body twitches as changes also happen to her insides. Her body is adapting to hold more air, and all of her insides are becoming stronger.

Even her skin is changing. It will become thicker and slick, like mine. I can already see that the color of her skin is different. It was a light peach color before, now it is taking on a bluish-green cast.

I run my hand up her ample hip and belly. She's very soft, but also thick and strong. This will be good to help protect her from danger and cold in her new underwater home.

I look over her body again and think about how pleased I am with her. She does not look like the females of my people, but despite the differences, I find her beautiful. I like her strength and softness. I'll enjoy mating with her. Several of my tentacles coil upon each other at the thought.

I carry her back to my home.

Every male Sea Guardian longs for the day that he scents his mate, bites her, and steals her away to his home. I've put much work into providing the best nest and home for my future mate as I can. I want her to be pleased when I bring her here.

I've made our home in the sunken remains of an old ship. The nest is in the captain's room because I like the large windows. They help protect us but also allow me to see any danger coming.

When I first came upon the ship, it was filled with furniture from the Elven. I've pushed most of that against the windows and to the other side of the room to help reinforce my nest.

I bring my female to the safest part of my nest, which is also where I sleep. I cradle her, coiled in my tentacles, while I wait for her to wake.

Until then, I study her. Her ears have become finned. Her gills look to be well formed and working well. Her finger and toe webs are also well formed. She's a mate fitting of a Guardian like me, and I puff my chest out with pride at my new mate.

I look at the cloud of long yellow hair that is floating around her head. Hair can be difficult in water. Those pompous Merfolk always have their hair billowing around their heads like this. It means they can't see anything that might be about to attack them. I gather her hair into one bunch, then separate it into three smaller bunches and braid it like I would braid tentacles. When I get to the end,

I realize that I'll have to tie off her hair with something because hair won't hold onto itself. I find a long strand of seaweed and use it to tie the end of the braid. Perfect. Now I can better see her delicate face.

I'm studying her face when she suddenly opens her eyes wide and begins screaming.

It is the change; it surprises her. I hold on tightly to her because in her panic, she has begun thrashing and hitting. I try to tell her to calm herself, but she won't stop screaming and fighting long enough to hear me. I continue holding her tightly as she shouts and squirms.

This eventually grows tiring. Why won't she let me help her? In frustration, I end up bellowing at her to be quiet. She goes still in my tentacles and stares at me with wide eyes. She looks terrified, which is not good. But at least she's no longer fighting me.

In an attempt to comfort her, I pull her close to my chest and stroke her cheek to soothe her. I say, "I'm honored to have such a strong female as a mate."

Just then she jolts away from my chest and I see her face fill with rage. Then she begins screaming and thrashing again.

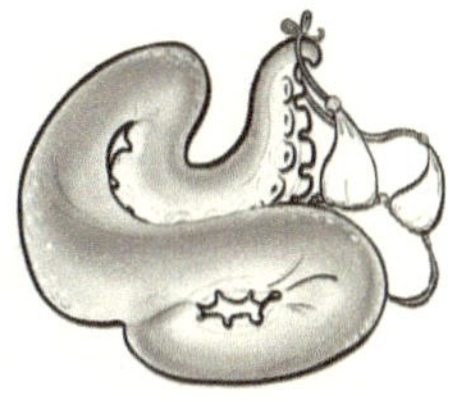

Chapter 3

I gasp as I jolt awake.

I frantically look around trying to make sense of my surroundings. Am I underwater? That's not possible. I don't understand.

Then all rational thought leaves me when I realize that the tentacle monster still has me. He's coiled around me, holding me with his tentacles. I scream and fight and even try to bite him again, but nothing works. He's so much stronger than me, and I'm not able to break away from him. I continue fighting though.

If some fucking monster is going to kill me, I'm not going to go down without a fight. I'm at least going to make it hard for him.

I continue fighting against him until my muscles are screaming from the effort. Just as I think I won't be able to go on, he drags me closer to him and yells in my face to be quiet.

I'm stunned into silence and go still against him. *He* yelled at *me* to be quiet! What the fuck?! He thinks I'm the one causing problems here?!

I float in front of him, staring at him. Then he drags me even closer, pressing my cheek gently against his chest. He runs a deadly looking webbed hand with terrifying, long, curved claws down my cheek as if he's comforting me. Then he says something about a *mate.*

Why did he say 'mate'? What the fuck?! Does he think I'm going to *mate* with him?! Is he fucking delusional?!

I immediately begin screaming and fighting him again with renewed force. "I'm not mating with a fucking octopus, you asshole!!"

He startles for just a moment. That moment is just enough for me to start to break out of his grip. I finally feel like I might be getting away from him when he bellows and pulls me back closer. He flings me over his shoulder and holds my arms and legs with tenacles. Then he drags me across...a room? Are we in a room? Underwater? What the fuck is going on here? I try to look back behind me to see where he's taking me, but I can't see around his stupid bulbous octopus head.

Suddenly he throws me forward, and my back hits metal bars. Metal bars—under water? What the fuck? I frantically look around and realize that it's a cage. He slams the door and bends a piece of metal around the bars so I can't open it and escape. I immediately grab the ends of the metal and try to unbend it, but it's no use. I'm not strong enough. Frustrated, I let go of it and look around me, then I realize I'm in some kind of diving cage for swimming with sharks.

What's happening? I don't understand any of this, and I'm beginning to panic. My ears start ringing and I feel dizzy. My heart is racing and I'm gasping for air. I feel like I can't breathe.

Then it hits me—how am I breathing? I realize then that my neck feels weird. I reach my hand up to my neck and freeze when I catch sight of my hand. Instead of my short, chubby fingers, I now have thin fingers with thick webbing between them. And instead of being pale, my skin has turned a soft blue-green. I lift my other hand to look at it, and it's the same. I frantically check my feet. They're even worse. My toes have grown much longer and webbing has grown between them. It looks they have turned into fucking flippers!

I'm panicking now. What happened? I reach my hands up to feel my neck, and there are gills. *Gills!* The realization that I now have gills completely breaks me. My stomach drops and my vision grows dark around the edges. No. This can't be happening. I feel my hands begin shaking and my muscles burn with adrenaline. I scream.

I look at the monster and shriek, "What did you do to me?" I beat on the bars with my hands and slam my shoulder against them, all while screaming at him to let me go. He just watches me. He isn't moving to let me go or apologizing; he just watches. Eventually, I tire myself out, cling to the bars of the cage, and cry.

Chapter 4

OCTHOGH'XU

This has not gone as I expected.

I expected to be coiled around her, both of us in the throes of ecstasy by now. Females long for their mate to scent them, claim them with their mating bite, then steal them away. Instead, she screams and rages at me. I don't understand. She should be honored that I've claimed her as my mate, but instead she's angry at me. She even called me an *octopus*! How dare she insult me!

Eventually she wears herself out, and then she just cries.

I watch her from my nest. She fought so hard that her lovely yellow hair has come loose from the braid I made, and it billows around her head. What do I do? Why is she angry? How do I make her not angry with me?

As she continues to softly cry, I decide to try to talk to her. I use my tentacles to quietly pull myself along to her.

Once I'm there, I hold my head high, clear my throat and say, "Female, I am the Guardian Octhogh'xu, I—"

She interrupts me with a dejected sigh. Without even looking at me, she quietly says, "What did you do to me?"

Startled that she's even talking to me, I pause for a moment and watch her. She finally looks at me. She wears the saddest, most defeated look I've ever seen. She touches the gills on her throat and then holds out her hands towards me. She sobs as she looks at them, "How—" She begins crying again and pauses so she can regain her composure. "How did you do this?"

She watches me, waiting for my answer.

I look into her human eyes. They are blue like the ocean, and full of sadness. Guilt begins to creep in. Does she not know about the mating bite? But she bit me first. Carefully I say, "You are my mate." Her face falls when I say this, but I continue, "I gave you my mating bite and claimed you as mine. It changed you so that you can live with me."

I watch as her face fills with rage again. "Your mating bite? You claimed me?" She's breathing heavily now. "I'm not a thing to be owned or taken! I'm a person! You can't just grab me and say I'm yours! You changed me?! You can't just change someone; you have to ask first!"

"This is how it is done. Your scent. I could taste you in the water. You were meant for me. You even bit me first, claiming me as yours."

She begins yelling again. "Meant for you!? I'm a person. You're an octopus. I can't be meant for you! I bit you because I was trying to get away!"

I snarl and fill with rage at that, then I bellow, "*I am not an octopus! I am a Guardian!*"

She startles at my rage and quiets for a moment. Then she smacks the bar of the cage. "I don't care! You have tentacles. I have legs. I'm not your mate! I'm not meant for you! I'm a human. Now change me back and take me back to where I came from!"

My mind reels; it feels as if I've been punched. She wants to go back? She's refusing me? I growl with my unhappiness. With a sneer I say, "Female, you are not going anywhere. *This* is your home now. I cannot undo my mating bite, and I would not if I could. You should be *honored* to be mated to a Guardian such as myself. I'm one of the strongest Sea Guardians in all of Ilsarius. I have fought hard to earn this territory and keep it safe. I deserve your respect! Countless females have tried to mate me for years, yet you call me an *octopus!?* You *will* treat me with the respect that I deserve, female!"

Rage and hatred burn in her eyes. "You fucking *octopus*."

I growl at her audacity. "You'll stay in there until you do."

Then I swim away. Away from my nest, the cage, and her.

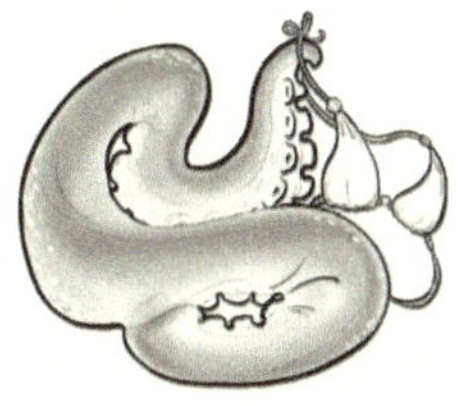

Chapter 5

Naomi

I seethe at the arrogance of that fucking octopus.

I shriek in anger and slam my hand into the bars repeatedly. Enough times that my hand hurts. I'm sure it will be bruised by the end of the day. Then I collapse into sobs and scream again.

He said he couldn't take the mating bite back. What am I going to do? Am I stuck like this? That thought just makes me cry harder.

Is this my life now? Kept in a cage by an octopus.

Then I suddenly realize—oh gods, he said mate...what else is he going to want? Is he going to want me to fuck him?

The horror of it settles over me. Oh gods, what is he going to do to me? My pulse starts to race, and I'm gasping for breath.

Okay, I have to calm down. I take a few deep breaths. I can't just sit down and cry, I need to get up and do something. I don't know what, but I need to try to figure something out.

I decide to look over the bars of the cage. Maybe something is damaged and I'll be able to find a way out.

I look over every inch of it. There are some areas that are crusted in barnacles, but once I pull those off, the metal underneath is fine.

Unfortunately, everything is still intact. In fact, it looks well made, and it's not even rusting. I huff in irritation—of course I couldn't get locked in a shitty shark cage.

Something nags at the back of my mind. Suddenly I realize what it is—aren't shark cages supposed to have escape hatches? I swear I've seen videos of them opening at the top. I look around again for other doors, but I can't find any. Then I realize that something is weird about this one. Every cage I've ever seen for shark diving had larger holes that the sharks couldn't fit through so people could take pictures without bars in their way. In some videos, a smaller shark's head will pop through the hole and into the cage, scaring the people inside. But this one doesn't have that.

Then I realize this is just a cage. It's not going to have escape hatches. It's meant to hold an animal or something...something like me.

I yell, "Shit! Shit shit shit!"

I hit the bar again, and my hand stings.

I remind myself to breathe again and tell myself that I can't panic. I have to stay calm and figure this out.

I try to think it through, and I realize that I'm not going to be able to get out of this cage until *he* comes back and lets me out, so I have to start playing nice. He's never going to let me out if I keep screaming at him.

I try to mentally prepare myself for being nice to him. I can be nice. It doesn't matter what he says, I just have to smile and nod. Then I can get him to let me out of here.

I try to settle in as best I can. Then, all I have to do is wait.

***

I wait for what feels like hours before I finally see a shape in the distance swimming towards me.

I briefly panic when I see it. What if it's something dangerous? What if it's someone else? But no, I feel a pull inside my chest. It feels like my heart knows it's him, and it's pulling toward him. I rub my chest because it's unsettling. But something about it also feels good. Something warm and comforting.

Out loud I tell myself, "Okay, Naomi...remember...be nice." I can do this.

I watch as he swims to the windows of this sunken ship. He slides through the broken-out window and comes into the room. He's carrying something over his shoulder, and he stops suddenly when he sees me watching him.

I stand up in my cage and say, "Um, hi. I think maybe we got off to a bad start. What would you think about a do-over?"

He frowns at me warily. "What is a *do-over*?"

I explain, "When we pretend to start over again and hopefully it will go better."

He simply replies, "No." Then he swims over to the cage and drops a netted bag in front of it.

I don't understand. Does he want to continue fighting and hating each other? Certainly he wants us to get along. "What do you mean...no?"

"We will fix this. We won't pretend," he says gruffly.

Uncertainly, I say, "Oh...uh...okay." I look down at the bag and realize it's full of wiggling crabs and oysters. Out of curiosity, I ask, "What's this?"

He glances at me with that one large eye. "I brought you food." He looks down, and I see a hint of something on his face. Regret, maybe. "To show you that I can care for you."

"Oh...." I don't really know what else to say, so I look down at the wiggling crabs again. He does know I need that cooked, right?

He opens the sack and grabs a large crab and rips a leg off. Then he holds it through the bars for me to take.

I stare at him in horror.

He huffs. "You won't eat the food I brought you? Is that not good enough for you either?" He practically growls.

I furrow my brow at his reaction. Wait, is he serious? Does he really think that I can eat raw crab? Rage boils up inside me.

I close my eyes and silently remind myself that I'm going to be nice. "I appreciate the food. It's just that I can't eat that raw. I need it cooked."

It's his turn to furrow his brow in confusion. "Cooked?"

"Yeah, cooked. Like on a fire." I say while I mime cooking with a skillet.

He snorts and raises his eyebrow while giving me a look that says he thinks I'm an idiot. He says, "A fire? You want a fire, here?" Then he gestures around us at all the water.

I look around and of course there's no fire for cooking. We're underwater. What am I supposed to do if there's no way to cook it?

He wiggles the crab leg at me again, and I cautiously take it from him. "I think I'm not supposed to eat this raw. It will make me sick."

He crunches down on a crab, taking a huge bite out of the side of a very alive, wiggling one, and I choke back a gag. He gives me a thoughtful look. "That was before, when you were all human. Now, thanks to my mating bite, you should be able to eat these."

I watch little bits of shell and meat float out of his mouth as he talks. We're underwater and he still manages to be a messy eater.

He gestures to the crab leg in my hand. "Eat."

I tentatively take a tiny bite of the meat hanging out of its shell, and I'm shocked when it is really good. It's sweet and succulent, better than any crab I've ever had at a restaurant. I moan at the flavor, then I quickly devour the rest of the meat. I was so hungry and didn't even realize it.

He smiles, and hands me another leg. I scarf it down quickly too.

Next, he hands me a whole crab through the bars of my cage. I savagely yank each of the legs off, then I take a huge bite out of the body and chew it up. Once I swallow that, I shove the other half in my mouth. Now I'm eating at least as messily as he is. He has a look of delight in his eye as I devour the legs. It's only then that I realize that I haven't been taking the shell off them. I'm eating them whole. For a moment I'm paralyzed with horror. I take a deep breath and exhale in defeat, then I go back to eating. Everything tastes so good, and I'm so hungry; I can't help myself.

I look at him expectantly once I'm done with that crab. He picks up an oyster and cracks it open with his claws. I watch as he picks out something shiny and tosses it to the side before he hands the oyster through the bars to me.

I gasp, "Was that a pearl?!"

He looks at the oyster and says, "Pearl?"

"Yes, a pearl. The little hard, shiny thing that you picked out of the oyster and threw on the ground." I point through the bars at where I can see the pearl shimmering.

He looks at it and shrugs. "You can't eat them, they just get in the way, so you throw them away."

I give a startled laugh when he says that. "All of your people do that?"

"Yes. Here, eat." He pushes the oyster through the bars to me. I take it and dump it into my mouth from the shell and moan at how delicious it is. I've only eaten oysters a few times and none of them ever tasted as good as this.

As soon as I swallow the oyster I say, "But they're valuable to humans. We use them for jewelry. Women get whole strings of them and wear them as a necklace. Pearls are timeless and elegant. Your people really just throw them away?"

He watches me for a moment, lost in thought. "Yes, we do." He cracks open another oyster and hands it to me. "Why do human women want them?"

I take it and say, "Because they're pretty. They're also hard for humans to find since we can't live under water, so that makes them rare."

After that, we eat in silence. He hands me crabs or oysters through the bars of the cage, and I devour them.

I thank him for the food when we're both full. Then I add, "I didn't realize how hungry I was. I ate so much."

He says, "It's probably the changes from my mating bite. You may require more food to live underwater now."

That statement is a harsh reminder of the situation I'm in. I don't understand how, but somehow I'd gotten lulled into a peaceful moment with him. I can't forget that I need him to let me go. I have to remember that he's the one that took me.

As meekly as possible, I say, "Hey, I was upset earlier with all of the...changes," I use one hand to gesture to my body, "and I didn't get your name. Can you tell me again?"

He gives me a wary look. "My name is Octhogh'xu. What's your name?"

I reply, "Naomi." Then I try to repeat his name in the same way that he said it, "Octoghtu." I mess up the second half of it though, I know I did. He gently corrects me, and I try again. But I still get it wrong. I laugh nervously, "Well, I can always just call you Octo as a nickname."

He gruffly says, "No. You'll practice saying it until you can say it correctly." Then he gathers up the remnants of our meal.

I'm stunned into silence. What the fuck? What an asshole. Fucking octopus.

He turns to look at me. "I must go now."

My heart drops and my breath catches. "Wait, what? You're leaving? But what about the cage? You can't just leave me locked in here." I can hear the edge of panic in my voice.

"I must go patrol my territory. I can already feel a lot of human activity on the beach that I found you on. You'll stay here."

"You can't just leave me here in a cage!" My voice hits a shrill note. I'm about to lose my shit. Rage and fear collide inside me. This fucking octopus better not leave me locked up like this.

He gives me an uncompromising look. "It's for your own good."

I slap the bars. "You fucking asshole! Don't you dare leave me here like this!"

He lets out a deep sigh and turns to swim off. As he's swimming away, he looks over his shoulder and says, "I'll be back later."

"Hey!! Let me out!! You can't keep me here!!" I scream at him as he swims away. I slam my hands over and over against the cage bars. "Get back here, you fucking octopus!!"

Rage consumes me, and I realize that there's no way I can be nice to him. I was doing really well...for a little while, at least. But this guy—no, he's not a guy—this *octopus* is a dick.

I continue to beat on the bars for who knows how long, then slump to the bottom of the cage. After that, I cry until I completely exhaust myself and fall asleep with one arm hooked around one of the bars, clinging to it.

Chapter 6

Octhogh'xu

I sigh as I swim away from the female...from Naomi. I can still hear her screaming. I also hear her call me an octopus again. I groan and run my hand down my face. How will I fix this?

I can sense the humans at the border of my territory. It's the same place I found Naomi, and that has me worried. I have to focus on this right now. I'll figure out how to fix things with Naomi later.

I swim to the border that's just shy of the beach. Our realm's border does not go all the way to the land because of humans; it stops at the edge of a large reef.

Our people have learned that humans fear harming coral reefs, so we've built up a reef along our border to help keep them and their machine boats out. This island in particular seems to attract a lot of human visitors, which is why such a strong Guardian is needed to protect it. Mostly, the humans just keep to the land and only go into shallow waters, but if they come out too deep, I handle them.

The amount of human activity that I sense right now is unusual, even for this spot. This is the same beach that I found Naomi on, and it makes me worried that this has to do with her. Would someone notice her going missing? Do humans notice when other humans go missing? What do they do when a human is lost?

As I near the beach, I can already tell that this'll be a problem. Even from this distance, I can see that there are two machine boats out, and people with suits, masks, and tanks swimming around each boat and around the ocean floor.

For a moment, I'm just impressed. I didn't know humans could achieve this. Then I'm concerned. The boats are right alongside the reef; they're close, but they've not yet crossed over it.

The border itself is a magical barrier and should deter most humans from crossing. However, some are more immune to magic than others. I'll have to deal with those humans if they cross the border.

I silently inch closer and lurk deep inside the reef. Here I'm able to camouflage my colors to match the reef and hide better.

It looks like the swimmers are searching for something. I take a deep breath and groan. This must be for Naomi.

I creep toward the edge of the reef, then in one explosive thrust of my tentacles, I dart towards the rocks surrounding the cove.

Beneath the surface of the water, there is a natural tunnel in the rocks. This tunnel exits at the base of several large rocks that hide me from humans on the beach.

I swim through the tunnel and climb onto the rocks. From my concealed perch, I see that this is a much bigger problem than I thought, even when I had only seen the swimmers. The alcove is swarming with humans.

Most of them aren't getting into the water, thank the Gods of the Sea. They're just talking to each other and appear to be searching the alcove. The quantity of humans is a problem. If many of them begin searching the water, then they'll probably start crossing our reef. That would be an invasion, and under those circumstances I'll have to send out a call for aid from my people and other Sea Guardians in the area. I would not be able to handle this many humans on my own. My hand absently goes to the small stone that all Sea Guardians wear around their necks.

A shrill female screech catches my attention and yanks me from my thoughts. It's a lot like the screeching that Naomi does. I search the humans trying to find the source of the terrible noise, and I see a female yelling at an older male. She's standing by Naomi's items that were on the beach when I took her, which are still laying in the same place they were when I grabbed her.

The female finishes yelling at the male and falls to the ground crying. A different male runs to her and embraces her.

I sigh. This *is* about Naomi. I survey all of the humans, both in and out of the water. They're searching for Naomi. My Naomi. They won't take her from me.

I slip back into the water and swim through the tunnel. I dart back to the reef and settle there to watch them from underwater.

They work for hours searching for someone that they will not find. I continue to watch them until I notice the sky changing from the setting sun. I need to go back to Naomi.

On my way back, I gather more crabs and oysters. She's likely to be very hungry by now.

As I swim back, I ponder if I should tell her about the people on the beach. Or maybe the female that was crying. Somehow, I think she would like to know this, but upon thinking about it, I realize that I can't tell her. She will demand to be taken to them at once, and when I tell her no, she will become even more enraged.

No, this is a secret that I must keep. She must never know.

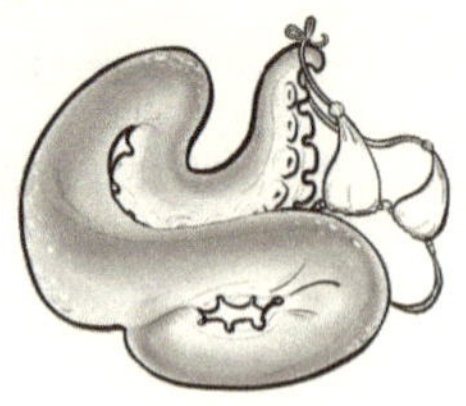

Chapter 7

Naomi

I sleep fitfully curled up on the floor of the cage with one hand holding onto a bar so I don't fucking float away. It's not comfortable at all, but I try to sleep anyway. Sleeping is better than being awake right now.

When I can't sleep, images of the parts of my life that I love flash through my head, haunting me. The things that I'm going to lose. Cindy and I laughing. My apartment—I wanted to get a cat. Having lunch with the other teachers that I'm friends with. The students that I connected with and genuinely enjoyed having in my class. Trips to the bookstore.

When I finally give up on sleeping, I just lay there staring out from between the bars of the cage. From where I'm lying, I can see the soft shimmering of the pearl that *he* threw onto the ground.

I'm out of ideas. I can't think of any way I can get out of here. I don't think there is anything I can do to convince him to let me go. I just have to wait until he decides to let me go.

I groan in frustration. Fuck, I don't even know what to call him. I can't even say his fucking name. I try to remember how he pronounced it. Octo-gh-th-zu? I don't think that was it.

I sigh feeling completely defeated. This is hopeless.

I lay there a little while longer. I eventually begin drawing little patterns in the sand under the cage. It's just a thin layer of sand over the boards that were once the floor of the ship, but it's somehow still soothing to draw in it.

When I look through the bars again, I notice a little fish swimming through the room. It's a colorful little fish and I try to lay as still as possible as it explores the room. It stops at the pearl and nibbles on it a few times before moving on to other things. Eventually it makes its way to the bars of the cage and nibbles at them. I slowly reach a hand out to see if it will come to me. After waiting for a few minutes, it finally makes its way to my hand and nibbles at the tips of my fingers. I giggle at the light tickling, which unfortunately startles the fish, causing it to swim away.

I sigh as I go back to laying on the floor of the cage.

I've always loved the ocean. I love fish and all the different creatures that live underwater. When I was a little girl, I would have done anything to live underwater. I wanted to be a mermaid.

It's sadly ironic now. Apparently, I do actually live underwater, only I'm stuck in a cage in a wrecked ship and I don't get to see any of the beauty down here.

I continue to lay there, wallowing in my self-pity. I'm starting to get hungry again, and I think about the crabs he brought me. I'm still horrified that I ate them without even taking the shell off.

Now that I'm thinking about it, how did I eat them with the shell on? I'm pretty sure my teeth couldn't bite through the shells. Oh no...my *teeth*. I bet my teeth have changed. I tentatively run my tongue over them, and they definitely feel a lot pointier. Fuck. Seriously?!

I reach a shaky hand toward my mouth and feel inside with my index finger. All of my teeth are sharp now. Not like razorblades or anything, but definitely pointed. Fuck.

I lay my head down to go back to wallowing in self-pity.

As I wallow, I look around the room I'm in. It looks like an old-world sunken ship. The kind that you see in pirate movies. Everything is covered in patches of barnacles. There's waterlogged furniture pushed up against the windows in a way that almost looks like a barricade. He must have been trying to make his home safer. Most of the windows are broken out, and one of those broken windows is how *he* left when he stormed off earlier, so I guess it makes sense that he would push something against the holes to help secure his home.

What is he trying to protect himself from? He's huge and very strong. What is someone like him afraid of? Sharks? Is he afraid of sharks? A shudder runs up my spine as a think about the possibility of a big shark circling the boat out there. But somehow, I doubt he's afraid of them.

A new fear slams into me. Oh gods, what if there's something bigger than him? Maybe some sort of kraken? Or maybe there are more people like him. What if he's one of the nice ones...and the others would just take me and force me to...

Fear has me in its icy grip, and I begin trying to look out the windows to see if I can make out any shapes or shadows swimming out there. My pulse is pounding so hard that I can hear it in my ears. I'm breathing heavier and I jump at any movement I see. The little fish swims back in through one of the windows and I gasp in surprise and nearly scream. It immediately swims away in a panic.

I remind myself to take a deep breath. I just need to calm down. I can stay calm and quiet, and nothing will find me.

Nothing will see me in here around all this furniture if I just stay quiet.

More fear builds in me when I realize that Octo said he scented me. Shit. Can ocean things smell really well? Will they be able to smell that I'm here? Then I remember that—oh gods—I've heard that sharks can smell the tiniest amount of blood in the water from miles away...or something like that.

I try to crane my head to see out the windows and watch for anything that might hurt me. It's then that I notice the water is getting darker, so the sun must be going down.

I suddenly realize that it's going to be pitch black down here.

Fear rolls through me in waves. My mind races. I can't be trapped down here in the ocean in complete darkness. I can't—I can't do it. I hate the dark. Another realization hits me—gods, what if something attacks me? I won't even be able to see it coming.

My heart is racing and my blood is thundering in my ears; I'm terrified now. I need him to come back. He can keep me safe. I need to get him to come back. I begin hitting the bars and screaming his name. Only, I can't say his name right. I'm on the verge of tears when I finally scream, "*Octo!*"

After what seems like hours of shouting his name, something darts through the broken window of the ship and suddenly he's in front of me. I scream when I see him.

He's urgently looking over me. "Female, what is it? What has happened?"

I'm frantic and sobbing. "It's getting dark. Please...I can't stay in here while it's dark. I can't. I can't. It's not safe. Please."

I reach through the cage for his arm, but he's too far away. I settle for a tentacle. I grab onto one and hold on.

I see him flinch when I touch him. I can tell he's shocked that I'm even touching him.

I beg and plead with him. "Please, don't leave me in here. I'm so afraid. I can't stay in there in the dark. Please. I can't see what's out there and something will get me. Please. I don't want to die in here." I'm sobbing and choking on my words at this point. "Please, Octo, please."

In a soothing voice, he says, "Shhh, it's okay, female. Stop crying." Then he reaches into the cage and begins unbending the metal that's holding the door closed. Once it's off, he opens the door.

I dart out and immediately swim into his arms. I wrap my arms around his neck, my legs around his waist, and bury my face against his chest. My cheek presses against a small stone that he wears on a chain around his neck. I cling to him.

I feel his body grow tense underneath me for a moment, then he relaxes and puts his arms around me. He whispers, "Ssshhhhhh," as he runs one of his clawed hands over my hair.

I'm still sobbing and trembling all over, but he continues to patiently comfort me.

He finally asks, "What scared you, female?"

I hiccup from crying then say, "It's going to be dark soon and I'm not going to be able to see anything down here. I wouldn't know if something was going to attack me. And I don't even know what's down here. What if there's a kraken or some sort of massive shark? They could smell me—they would—like you did. Then they would attack me, and I would never see it coming. Just like—just like I never saw you coming." I sob on the last sentence.

He looks at the cage and I see some sort of emotion flash across his eye. Then he says, "I'm sorry. I shouldn't have left you in there for so long. I didn't mean to be gone as long as I was."

I hiccup again and nod.

"But...you should be able to see enough in the dark to know if something is going to attack you." He uses his fingers to gently tilt my head back and forth; I let go of him and begin floating next to him while he studies my eyes.

Then he nods as if he was correct. "Yes, your eyes have a shine to them. You'll be able to see in the dark as other underwater creatures can."

I don't even know how to react to that. I'm equal parts relieved and horrified. My eyes have a shine to them? Like a cat? All I manage to say is, "Oh."

He gives me a small smile, then says, "Are you hungry? I brought more food."

At the mention of food, I realize how famished I am. My stomach growls and I sniff then say, "Yes."

He gives me a sad smile. "Come." He uses his tentacles to crawl toward the other side of this broken cabin.

Watching him crawl away from me, I realize that he has let me out. I'm free. Not just out of the cage—he's not even holding me. I could swim away! I take a moment to look around the cabin, and my gaze settles on the windows. All I can see outside of them is never-ending blue that is steadily getting darker.

No, I'm not free. I can't leave, and he knows it.

I look back at him and watch as he leans down to open his netted bag of food. I'm stuck here.

He pulls a crab from the bag and stands back up straight. He watches me for a moment. Then holds the crab out to me. "Do you want?"

Frustration is all I feel because, dammit, yes, I do want it. I'm starving. I cautiously swim over to him and take it out of his hand while I float next to him. Softly, I say, "Yes, thank you."

I hold it and watch him bend back down and grab another crab out of the bag. He raises it to his mouth and takes a huge bite, then looks at me as he chews and says, "Eat."

I do exactly that. I take a huge bite out of it, and it's just as delicious as the crabs were earlier. I don't even care that it wasn't dead when I took my first bite, or that it's raw. I don't care that it's still in its shell. It's the most amazing thing I've ever eaten. I finish that crab quickly and he hands me another. I immediately take a bite out of it and begin chewing. We end up eating quietly, him handing me something else to eat as soon as I finish what I have.

Once we are done, he picks up the netting and folds it until it fits into a pouch he has strapped to his waist. Then he looks at me and just watches me.

I stare out the windows; it's getting rapidly darker now. When I look back at him, he's still watching me like he doesn't know what to do with me. I'm overwhelmed with anxiety because I don't know what will come next.

Finally, I can't take the silence anymore. "Now what?"

I see him quickly glance toward the cage behind me, then he looks back at me. He says, "We sleep."

"But—"

"You choose. Do you want to sleep in the cage, or"—he gestures to his nest—"do you want to sleep in my nest with me?"

Fear floods my body. I glance at the cage. I can't sleep there, in the dark, alone. Then I look at his nest. But I also can't sleep there, with *him*. My heart starts pounding so hard that I can hear it in my ears, and I can tell I'm starting to breathe faster. There's a strange fluttery almost ticklish sensation in my neck—in my gills. If I weren't underwater, I know I would be sweating. Oh gods, how do I choose?

He must be able to sense my fear because he raises his hands in a calming gesture and says, "Just sleep. I will not force you to mate with me."

I study his face for a moment. Then I nod, and quietly say, "The nest then."

He nods and crawls to the nest, settling in. I haven't moved at all. I'm just watching him.

He looks up at me and gestures for me to come to him, so I cautiously swim toward him. I swim to his side, and he says, "Lay down, get comfortable."

I try to swim to the ground and sit down, but I just float. I keep having to push myself back down because I start floating away. I throw my hands up. "How am I supposed to sleep if I keep floating away from everything?"

He looks at me for a moment, then reaches a couple of tentacles up to me. One of them wraps around my waist and pulls me down toward him. It deftly tucks me into his side. The other wraps around an ankle to help hold me in place. A third one coils under my head as a makeshift pillow and then loops down my back to help keep me anchored there.

It's sort of alarming being cuddled by my kidnapper, but it's also really comfortable. It's so much more comfortable than I have been all day. I easily close my eyes and drift off to sleep.

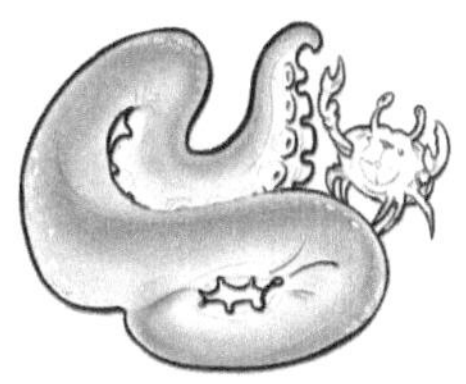

Chapter 8

Octhogh'xu

My mate is curled up next to me. Her scent permeates the water as she sleeps, and I long to reach out and touch her. I don't dare to do it though. She would surely be angry if I did. I don't dare to even move for fear of making her angry.

Instead, I focus on the tentacles that are holding her, especially the one she's resting her head on. She has tucked her face into the one cradling her head, and I can feel her lips resting against my skin. Several of my other tentacles twist around each other as I feel her lips moving slightly in her sleep. The brush of them against my skin is exquisite torture.

I can feel my cock wanting to extrude from its pocket, and I quietly groan. I can only imagine how enraged she would be if that happened.

I curl one of my tentacles into a knot and use it to press against my cock pocket in hopes of stopping it from extruding, but the tip of it already feels swollen and sensitive. If I continue thinking about it, there is going to be no way to stop it.

I try to distract myself several times, but all I can do is think about her.

Suddenly she wiggles and lets out a groan, then shifts so that her leg is thrown over one of my tentacles, trapping it between her strong thighs.

To my horror, my cock forcefully extrudes from my cock pocket. My tentacle was still tightly knotted and pressing against it. When my cock suddenly extrudes, my tentacle wraps around it, unintentionally stroking it tightly. The shock and pleasure of it causes me to groan loudly.

Naomi stirs, then jerks awake and sits up quickly.

She sounds frightened when she asks, "What happened? What's wrong?"

Hoping she won't notice my hard cock, I quickly respond, "Nothing. Just a dream." I try to pat her to get her to lay back down and go to sleep.

Her eyes roam over my body, looking for injuries. I try to cover my cock with my tentacles, but without being able to curl in the ones that are holding her, she has a perfect view of my hard cock.

I see her eyes lock onto it and then she gasps. "Is that...? What are you doing?" Then her voice grows accusing, "Oh my gods, were you jerking off while I was snuggled up to you?"

I don't know this *jerking off* phrase that she used, but I feel certain that it means stroking my cock.

She backs away from me, but she quickly reaches as far as my tentacles allow. When she realizes that she can't get away from me, she screeches and practically growls, "Let go of me."

I give her a pleading look and hold my hands out, begging her to calm down. "No, no—it's not—it's not what you think."

Her face is full of rage. "Not what I think? How is it not what I think? It certainly looks like you were jerking off while watching me sleep!"

I beg more, "No. It's not. I wasn't. It just...I did not mean for this."

"Bullshit. You were getting off while I was sleeping next to you! I swear, all men are the same, even octopus ones."

More forcefully now, I say, "NO! Naomi…please." I scrub my hand down my face. "I was not pleasuring myself while you were sleeping. You were snuggling up to my tentacles. My cock just…reacted. It extruded and surprised me." I sigh and slump in defeat. "I did not want to make you angrier at me. I tried, but I couldn't stop it."

She's gone still and is watching me warily. I don't know if this is a good thing, but at least she isn't yelling at me anymore.

Finally, after what feels like days, she says, "Extruded? What does that mean?"

I groan. Gods of the Sea, please kill me. As if this could get worse.

I cautiously say, "It comes out of my…out of the cock pocket."

Her eyes get wider. "Cock pocket? What's that?"

I groan again and give her a helpless look, but what I see on her face is curiosity, not rage. I say, "It's where my cock is stored, inside me, until I'm ready to mate."

Her eyes get even wider, and she raises her eyebrows. "Oh wow. You keep it on the inside?"

Confused I ask, "Do human males not do this?"

She shakes her head "No. Theirs dangle on the outside."

I'm horrified. Dangle on the outside? "But what if they get into a fight?"

She snickers. "They have to be careful not to get hit. They also wear pants, that at least protects it some. If they're doing something like sports or training for fighting, they wear a thing called a cup. It protects them."

I think I have heard of this thing called a cup. Don't humans drink out of them? But they also use them to protect their cocks? That seems strange.

I'm still pondering this when she says, "Um...can I see?"

I'm stunned. She wants to see my cock?

Her cheeks turn pink. "I just...I've never seen one like that. I was just curious—it's not like—I'm just curious."

I tentatively lift my tentacles so she can see. Her eyes go wide as she looks at it, and my cock is painfully hard. I watch in horror as a little bit of seed slides out and then floats away to mix with the water.

She watches all of this, then she finally says, "It's a lot different than a human's." She continues to stare at it. After another minute, she murmurs, "It's so...thick." Her cheeks turn even pinker, then she abruptly sits up and looks away.

I catch a hint of her scent; it's stronger now. Could she be...aroused?

She quickly says, "Well, I think all of that was just a misunderstanding. I'm sorry I yelled at you. We should go back to sleep now." She lays back down and arranges herself the way she had when she first fell asleep. "Goodnight, Octo." Then she closes her eyes.

My voice is husky when I say, "Goodnight, Naomi."

Then I'm left with nothing but my thoughts and a very hard cock.

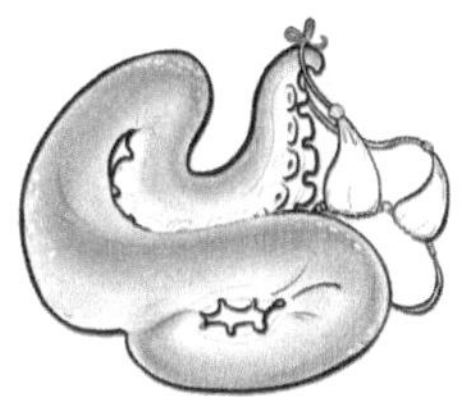

Chapter 9

NAOMI

I lay there with my eyes closed, pretending to be asleep.

My mind is racing—did I just get turned on by an octopus dick? I don't know what happened. He was embarrassed and not acting like an asshole for once. It was also kind of sweet how stressed out he was. He really didn't want me to think he was taking advantage of the situation.

And then I saw his cock. And wow...it's big and thick, but it's not like a human dick. It's tapered and smooth with a significant swell in the middle of the shaft.

All I could think about was how much I wanted to touch it. I desperately wanted to wrap my hand around it and stroke it.

I have a brief mental image of what it would look like sliding into me, and I squeeze my thighs together tightly. I can already tell that I'm wet.

I don't understand what's going on. I cannot seriously be getting turned on by an octopus guy. This must be Stockholm Syndrome. That's the only reasonable explanation for it.

Certainly, they can do something about Stockholm Syndrome. I can go to lots of therapy or something. I remind myself to breathe. It's all going to be fine. This is fixable.

For now, I just need to get some sleep. I'm not feeling very tired, but if I just lay here long enough with my eyes closed, I'll fall asleep.

So that's what I do.

Eventually I do drift off to sleep.

***

I'm startled when I wake up later. I have no idea where I am. Then everything from the day before comes rushing back to me. Oh gods, that was all real.

I go to move my arm and realize that I'm pressing against metal bars, instead of tentacles.

The cage. I'm back in the cage again, and I've floated up to the top of it, so I'm pressing against the top bars.

I turn in the water until I'm upright, then I look around the room. Octo is on the other side working on something that looks like a long metal spear. Is he sharpening it? I look at it more closely. It is a spear—but it's not what I would imagine a creature like him to have. I would expect an old, rusted harpoon or something, but this is a gleaming metal spear. It's actually quite modern looking—and brutal. The blade itself is at least as long as my forearm, probably longer.

Carefully, I say, "Hey...Octothetu?" I already know that I said it wrong. This feels hopeless. I'm never going to learn how to say his stupid name, but at least I tried. It's not like he's even trying to teach me. Just saying it over and over isn't teaching. Fucking stubborn octopus.

"It's Octhogh'xu," he says.

I glare at him. "Right. So, why am I in the cage again? I thought we were past this." I'm trying really, really fucking hard to stay calm right now, but we can't be back to this. I can't stay in here.

He stops working on his spear and looks at me. "It has to be this way."

My heart drops. No, it can't be this way. I sound distinctly whiny when I say, "Why? Why does it have to be this way."

He lets out a resigned sigh. "I have to go patrol my territory and can't leave you here alone."

I gasp. He's going to leave me here alone again. Probably for hours again. "No, please. Please don't leave me in here. I—I can come with you. I can help." I can feel the tears behind my eyes threatening to spill out.

He crawls over to the cage and gives me a sad look. Then he sticks one hand through the bars and strokes my cheek. I try not to flinch as he does it. "This is the only way I can keep you safe. It's too dangerous for you to come with me."

"No please, Octo. I can stay here. I'll stay right here in this room. Just please don't leave me in this cage again." I sound so weak begging like this, and I'm deeply ashamed. But I can't stay in here.

He shakes his head. "No, Naomi. You would try to leave. You have to stay in the cage."

I actually do start crying now. Then I get angry. I hit the bar with my hand. "Fuck you, Octo! Fuck you!"

He sighs, resigned to this fight. He knew this was going to go this way. That's why he snuck me in here while I was still asleep.

"I'm a person, Octo. You can't just leave me in a cage all the time!" I yell. "You know what, you're fucking right, I would leave. I would leave in a heartbeat. Why would I stay here? You kidnapped me, Octo!"

Octo picks up his spear and then looks at me. Still with the same resignation, he says, "I must go protect my territory. I will not leave you for long. I'll bring food when I come back."

As he turns and begins to swim off, I practically wail, "No! Don't leave me trapped here! Please, Octo! Don't do this!"

I see him pause for a moment and look back at me. Then he says, "I'm sorry, Naomi," and swims away.

I scream in anger and frustration, "No! Get back here, you fucking octopus!"

Then I break down and cry. I hold onto the bars, leaning into them, and sob.

Chapter 10

I swim away from her, and her sobs follow me. They haunt me. I feel our bond aching in my chest. But I can't let her out. It is not safe enough for her to come with me. She would see the people hunting for her. She would know how to get home. She said it herself—she would leave if she could.

No, she must stay locked up when she's not with me. It makes my hearts ache, though. I don't want to treat my mate like this, but I don't know how to fix it.

As I near the reef, I pause for a moment to clear my head. I run my hand over my face. If I'm going to protect my territory, I need to focus. I'll think about how to fix things with Naomi when I'm done here. For now, I need to only think of the humans and what they're doing.

Once I feel like I'm calm enough to continue, I swim into the reef. I survey the water leading to the beach, and there are still humans swimming from boats. They're still hunting for Naomi.

When it's safe, I quickly dart into the underground tunnel so that I can check on the beach. Once I get to the rock that I'm able to spy from, I groan when I see even more humans on the beach. This is not good. I'd hoped that there would be less humans, not more.

I watch for a while, but I eventually grow tired of watching them, and my thoughts shift back to Naomi.

How am I going to fix things with her? She's my mate; she cannot hate me forever...can she? I silently make my way back to the reef, my thoughts still consumed with her.

Once I'm safely hidden in the reef, I notice some of the humans swimming toward my hiding place. I ready my spear.

They come to the edge of the human lands and look out over the reef. They seem to be communicating with each other, but I cannot hear what they're saying.

One of them points back in the direction that I just came from, and I groan. One of them must have seen me as I swam back to the reef. I was too distracted. I should have paid better attention.

I continue to watch them until they turn back and swim toward the boat.

I must be more careful. I cannot let Naomi distract me. If they were to harm me, Naomi would be trapped. She would die. There is too much at stake now, I must focus.

I watch the humans for a little while longer. The ones that seemed to have spotted me don't come back. They climb into their boat and leave. Good. I don't need more to worry about.

I swim back toward my home and gather food for Naomi as I go.

As I collect food, the idea that Naomi would be trapped if something happened to me keeps running through my mind. I need to figure out a better way. I can't keep locking her in that cage every time I leave. Not only because she could get trapped, but she will never quit hating me if I continue locking her in there.

I must tell someone else about her.

I finish collecting the food and swim back to my home. I feel the tug of our bond as soon as I get close. I brace myself for Naomi's mood when I swim into my nest.

She watches me swim into the room without saying anything, however, she's floating in the middle of the cage glaring at me. I sigh and set the bag down, then go to her.

She continues to glare at me while I unwrap the metal holding the door closed. At least she isn't crying anymore.

As soon as I open the cage, she swims out. She stops beside me and just floats there, glaring at me with her arms across her chest.

"You're an asshole, Octo. A fucking asshole octopus."

I sigh again. "I'm sorry I locked you up. I don't want to, but I have to keep you safe somehow."

She just continues glaring at me.

"I'll find another way, a better way. One that isn't this."

She cooly says, "I have an idea, it's shockingly simple...I could just *come with you*."

"No, it's too dangerous."

She groans in frustration. "What's too dangerous? What are you so afraid of?"

I'm afraid she's going to swim straight back to that beach and to the humans, but I can't tell her that. Instead, I say, "The ocean is full of predators that wouldn't think twice about eating you. Do you know how to prevent a shark attack?"

She pauses to think about it. "No. But what if I just stay with you."

I shake my head. "What if I have to defend my territory from a human? If humans caught you, do you know what they would do with you?"

"Humans? But I'm a human."

I shake my head again. "You aren't a human anymore. If they saw you, they would capture you and take you away, never to be seen again."

She scrunches her forehead and furrows her brow. "Capture? Have they captured any of your people before? Certainly not, something like that would have been all over the news. I would know about it."

I give her a dubious look. "You would?

She thinks for a second. "Yeah, that would have been everywhere. Everyone would be talking about it."

"But humans *have* taken my kind before."

She gasps, "But...I...oh my gods! Do you mean that humans know about you?"

"Yes."

She just stares at me in stunned silence for a moment. "But...I mean...who...who took them? What happened to them?"

I shrug my shoulders. "No one sees you again if you're taken by humans. You were a human, what do you think happens to them?"

She gets a dark look on her face. "Nothing good." Then she's quiet and obviously lost in thought. Finally, she says quietly, "Have you known anyone that has been taken?"

"Yes, my father's brother."

She gasps again, then reaches out as if she's going to touch me, but she pulls her hand back as if she rethinks it. "Oh, Octo, I'm so sorry. That's terrible."

"It's Octhogh'xu."

She gives an exasperated huff. "Really? I'm trying to be nice."

"You need to learn how to say my name."

She sighs heavily, then goes quiet.

I go over to the bag of food and pull out a crab and hold it out to her. "Eat."

She swims towards me, takes it, and tears into it greedily. Once she's done with that crab, I hand her another.

She eats well, and I enjoy watching her eat. Even though she fights me on everything, at least she lets me care for her by feeding her.

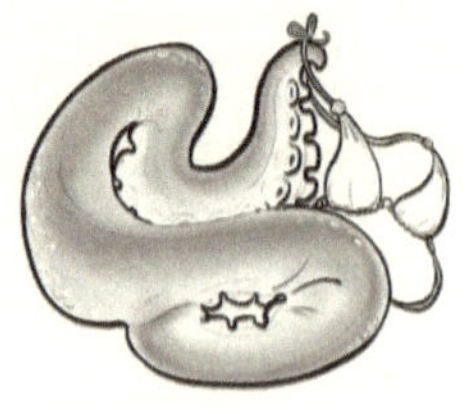

Chapter 11

Naomi

Octo and I eat in silence. The food he brings still tastes amazing, but I'm lost in thought about what he told me.

Humans have captured his kind before. That means that someone out there knows that these people exist. Since the public has never known about all of this, I'm assuming some sort of secret government agency deals with it.

Gods, I don't even want to know what kind of horrific things the human governments could be doing to the people they capture. I'm sure its horrible experiments that end in the person's death.

He's right though; if they saw me the way I am now, they would capture me too. I would be taken away, and it wouldn't matter that I'm human or that I'm a citizen of their country—they would experiment on me just the same.

I look at Octo. "You said the mating bite can't be undone, right? The way my body has changed...it can't be changed back to what I was? There isn't some sort of magic that can undo it?"

He sighs heavily and I see his shoulders slump a little. "No, it cannot."

I nod and go back to quietly eating, lost in thought. I feel like I should be devastated by that confirmation, but I'm not. I've had a lot of time to think while I've been trapped in that cage. He'd already told me that I couldn't be changed back. He was angry at that time, but I think I believed him. The truth is, I think I knew from the moment that I realized I had gills that there was no going back. Maybe I'm starting to accept this. Maybe it's time for me to start trying to do something or learn about this world.

Octo pulls me from my thoughts when he says, "I...," he pauses to rub his hand down his face, "I ought to apologize to you. I did not think when I took you. I did not consider how you would feel. In our world, when a male scents his mate, he steals her and gives her his mating bite. Females expect this, and long for this. But you are not a Guardian, and humans must do things differently. I'm not sorry that you are my mate. I think you're a good, strong mate, but

I'm sorry that I scared you. I ought to have considered that you wouldn't understand."

I feel a lump form in my throat, and my eyes are prickling like I'm going to cry. He's *apologizing* to me.

I don't even know what to say, I just quietly nod and whisper, "Thank you."

He nods, and we both go back to eating in silence.

I finally break the silence. "Can...um...can you show me more of this world? If this is going to be my home, I would like to see it and learn about it."

He looks at me with surprise. "You want to learn about my world?"

I nod. "Also, if you can teach me what to do about a shark, that would make me feel a lot better."

He chuckles. "Humans always seem afraid of sharks. I've heard plenty of humans screaming about sharks when there was no shark there."

I laugh too. "That's not surprising. There was a movie a long time ago about a shark that hunted and attacked people. It would take down whole boats. It probably made everyone more afraid. Plus, people do get attacked sometimes."

"What is a *movie*?"

I didn't even think about the fact that he wouldn't know what that was. "It's a story that you can watch on a television screen."

He furrows his brow and gives me a confused look.

"Have you ever seen humans on the beach looking at little rectangles that glow on one side? They're about this big." I use my hands to mime how big a phone is and what it would look like holding one.

He nods, "Yes, I have seen this. I have often wondered what they were staring at for so long."

"It plays videos on it. It's moving pictures of something happening."

He furrows his brow again.

I realize then that he wouldn't know what a picture is. Or a drawing, or a painting. How do I describe it to someone that has no way of capturing pictures? I finally say, "It's a story told from one person to another. It's about a huge shark that kills tons of people."

He shakes his head. "That sounds like it is just meant to scare people. Sharks don't actually act like that." He gets a sheepish look then says, "Most here are small and wouldn't bother you. I just mentioned sharks because I wanted you to be too scared to go with me."

I frown. "Of course you did."

He gives me a regretful look. "Still, sometimes big ones do come into my territory. It would be good for you to know what to do if you encounter one. It is not hard to deter one. They have very sensitive snouts. If they swim at you, you can usually push them away so they'll just swim past you. But if one opens its mouth to bite, just hit it on the snout. It should swim away then. I'll take you to some small sharks and you can practice."

"Practice?! Won't they hurt me?"

He scoffs. "No, they're too small to want to bite us. We are more dangerous than they are."

I think about it for a minute. "Okay, that sounds good...I guess. Is there anything else that I should be worried about hurting me? What about other Guardians?"

He shakes his head. "No, the other Guardians will scent that we are mates. They'll know that we are bound to each other, so they will not bother you."

I'm not sure if I believe that. "They won't try to take me anyway? Why would they care about the bond?"

He gives me a surprised look. "Have you not noticed? We are drawn toward each other. Our hearts are connected. I would be able to feel where you were and would hunt you down and kill the Guardian that took you. It's too risky for a Guardian to steal another Guardian's mate once they have received a mating bite."

"Oh."

"Can you feel it when I'm returning home? It's like a pull in your chest." He rubs the center of his chest, right over his sternum.

I absently rub my chest in the same spot. "Yes, I can."

He smiles. "Good. That is our mating bond. It will keep you safe from any other Guardians trying to claim you as their mate."

Okay, so I'm safe from sharks and other Guardians. "What about giant sea creatures, or krakens, or something like that?"

Octo furrows his brow. "Giant sea creatures? Kraken? There is nothing large here that you need to be afraid of, Naomi."

I sigh. I feel like an idiot. Of course there aren't krakens. "Sorry...more stories."

He watches me for a moment, then he very gently says, "There are dangerous things in the very deep, dark waters of the ocean, but we don't go there. We could not survive there. And those things could not survive here. You don't need to worry about creatures of the sea."

But I don't understand, he keeps telling me he has to keep me safe. "Then why do you keep saying I'm not safe and you have to keep me safe?"

He sighs. "Humans. Humans are not safe. I'm trying to protect you from humans."

"Oh." I watch him for a moment, but I don't know what to say. He's right, of course. Humans are the most dangerous creatures out there.

By this point, we are done eating and he begins folding up his net to put it away. He looks at me, and I can tell he's going to say something that he knows will piss me off.

"Just say it. You need me to go back into the cage, don't you?" I say dejectedly.

"Yes."

I groan loudly and bury my face in my hands.

He puts his hands out in a calming way, "You will only need to stay in there for a little bit. I promise. I think I know a way to fix this."

"How?" I demand.

"I can't tell you until I know for sure." he explains.

"No, I don't want to go back in there. Take me with you."

It's his turn to groan.

"Is it dangerous?"

He shakes his head. "No."

I cross my arms over my chest. "Then why can't I go with you? You said you would show me this world."

He sighs and says, "I will, but it will be better if I do this alone. I promise it won't be long."

I'm being a brat, I know I am, but I don't want to go back into that cage.

"Naomi, please. Go into there this last time. I will not take long, and I promise I'll take you out and show you everything you want to see."

I pause and think about it for a minute. He looks anxious, and I think he's telling the truth. He's trying. Maybe I need to give just a little and try too.

I sigh. "Dammit. Fine." I turn and swim into the cage. "You better not be lying to me, Octohutu."

He chuckles and shakes his head as he bends the metal around the bars to lock me in.

"Hey, I'm trying. Your name is really hard to say."

He says, "It's Octhogh'xu. Say it like this, Oc-tho-gh-shoo."

I roll my eyes dramatically, but I give it a try. "Oc-tho-gh-shoo...Octhogh'xu." I gasp because I think I said it right.

When I look at him, he smiles warmly at me. "Good, that is correct."

He studies my face for a moment, then says, "I'll be back soon. I will not be gone as long as I normally am. Don't fret."

I nod. "I'll try, Octhogh'xu." I know I've said it correctly again.

He smiles, then turns and swims off.

I anxiously watch him swim away. All I can do is hope he isn't lying to me.

Chapter 12

Octhogh'xu / Octo

For the first time, I swim away from Naomi feeling a little bit of hope. That hope turns to anxiety when I realize I must do.

I swim to the outer edge of my territory, and into the neighboring territory. The Guardian, Ovaggd'tho, is a friend of mine from when we were young. He's mated to a female named Xaiolpa. Ovaggd'tho and I have always helped each other, I'm hoping he can help me as he has more experience with mating bonds.

As I near the cave he has made his nest in, I feel my hearts beating faster. What will he think of my mating with Naomi?

I stop just shy of the cave. I'm suddenly overwhelmed with doubt. When Ovaggd'tho finds out about the cage... Maybe this is a bad idea.

Just then, Xaiolpa swims out of the cave with a warm smile and says, "Octhogh'xu! I thought I scented you! Ovaggd'tho is just inside the cave." She turns and calls his name.

Ovaggd'tho comes swimming out and greets me with a big hug and a clap on the back. Then he gives me a concerned look. "Is something wrong?"

I sigh. "I need your help. I have made a mess of something, and I don't know how to fix it."

"Oh no, is it that female again? The one that's always trying to snag you as a mate? Such a pushy female. I can have Xaiolpa speak with her." He glances at her, and Xaiolpa nods eagerly. Then he pauses and gives me a curious look. "Your scent is different."

"I...well...I have taken a mate."

Xaiolpa gasps happily, and Ovaggd'tho roars a cheer. "That is wonderful news! Who is it, is it someone we know?"

I hesitate, then say, "No. She's—she was a human."

They glance at each other and then both stare at me at a loss for what to say. Finally, Ovaggd'tho says, "A human. But...where...how a human?"

I shake my head. "Her scent...it just called to me. I was patrolling near the beach that they like so much, and I scented her in the water. I knew instantly that she was my mate."

Ovaggd'tho's face softens into a smile. "That's wonderful, I'm happy for you."

I give him a sad look. "But I have made a mess of it. I took her...stole her from the beach." I wince as I remember. "I gave her my mating bite and took her to my home. But this is not how humans do it. She says I took her against her will. She hates me."

Ovaggd'tho looks surprised. "Humans don't take mates in the same way as us?" His face darkens as he thinks about it. "I imagine this must have been very frightening for her then. Let us help you. Maybe Xaiolpa can talk to her and help her release her anger."

Xaiolpa beams. "I would be happy to speak with her."

I don't have the hearts to tell them about the cage, so I don't.

Ovaggd'tho smiles at me. "Don't worry, we will make this right. Come, let's go to your nest."

They swim off in the direction of my home.

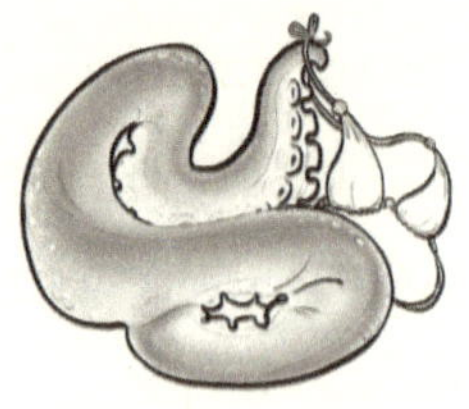

Chapter 13

Naomi

I grow impatient as I wait in the cage. This is the problem with it...well, one of the problems. I have no sense of how long it's been since he left. Every minute feels like hours.

Before long, I feel the tell-tale tug in my chest letting me know he's near. I feel my heart beat faster as I watch for him through the broken window.

When he's close enough for me to see, I realize that he's not alone. Two other...uh...Guardians are with him. Octo quickly swims through the window first and swims straight for the cage. He spreads himself in front of it like he's guarding me from them. Anxiously I reach my arm through and rest my hand on his shoulder.

The other two swim through the broken window and stop short just inside the ship. It's another male Guardian and a female Guardian. The female gasps when she sees me. The male looks angry.

He looks at me, then says, "Octhogh'xu! You locked her in a cage! This is no way to treat your mate!"

Octo shakes his head. "No, you don't understand. I'm trying to keep her safe."

The other male's tentacles flare in agitation, "No, this is not the way. How long has she been in there? How long have you been mated?"

Octo hangs his head and slumps his shoulders. "Since yesterday morning."

The female swims forward with a shocked look on her face. "Octhogh'xu! I can't believe you would do this!" She looks over Octo's shoulder at me. "Are you okay, human?"

I nod, unsure of what's happening, but I'm suddenly afraid they'll take me from him. "He lets me out! He just puts me in here when he has to leave." *Hello, Stockholm Syndrome.*

The male practically bellows, "No!! You are better than this, Octhogh'xu!"

Octo turns to me and looks utterly defeated, and my heart aches for him. He removes the metal holding the door closed, and I swim out but stay at his side. I wrap both hands around his muscular arm and cling to him.

He gives me a look of surprise, then he looks back to the other two. "I did not know how to keep her safe. And she was so angry that I took her. She fought so hard. She even bit me. I could not stand to lose her."

The other male just shakes his head then he comes forward and clasps Octo on the shoulder. "We are your friends; you ought to have come to us sooner. We would have helped." Then he looks at me with laughter dancing in his eyes. "Did you really bite him human?"

I nod.

Octo points to the spot on his neck; you can still see the mark.

The other male roars in laughter. It startles me and I grip onto Octo tighter. The male gives Octo a hard clap on the back and says, "You picked a feisty one, didn't you? And was that with her human teeth, before you bit her?"

Octo nods.

The other male laughs harder. "That is impressive, little human."

I smile cautiously. These are his friends?

The female comes forward and says, "I'm Xaiolpa, and this is my mate, Ovaggd'tho. We are so happy to meet you, although I'm very sorry Octhogh'xu handled all of this the way he did." She gives Octo a pointed look, and I hear him sigh.

I finally find my voice and say, "Hi, I'm Naomi."

She smiles. "Naomi, what a beautiful name. And you're such a beauty, so exotic!"

I grin back at her. "Thank you."

That statement has to be absolute lunacy coming from her though. Where Octo and the other male are all bulky brute strength, she's slim and muscular and absolutely gorgeous. She has large golden eyes, plump lips, and love-ly red and pink skin. Her bulbous octopus...uh...mantle bounces behind her creating the impression of bouncy hair. Her tentacles are longer and more slender than the thick tentacles that Octo and the other male have. She has the soft curve of small breasts that are very similar to human breasts, including nipples. I'm suddenly surprised and slightly embarrassed when I realize that I've basically been staring at her naked breasts. No one else seems to pay much attention to the nudity, though.

As I look between the three of them, I realize that they're all wearing a necklace made of some type of chain with a small stone on it. I'd noticed it on Octo, but I thought it was just something he wore for aesthetics, but now I realize it must have some sort of cultural significance.

The female, Xaiolpa, clasps her hands together. "So, how can we help you two? How can we help make this right? Assuming Octhogh'xu stops locking you in a cage."

Octo sighs, "I don't want to lock her in there anymore. I don't know how to keep her safe, though. She isn't from this world. She doesn't know how to stay safe here. And I have humans encroaching on my border. I need to keep an eye on them, but I can't take her with me. What if a human got her?"

Everyone sobers at that reminder.

Xaiolpa says, "Well, she could come stay with me while you protect your territory, or I could come here and stay with her."

I nod enthusiastically.

Octo gives me a cautious look then says, "Only if she promises not to try to swim away."

Xaiolpa tsks. "Well maybe she wouldn't need to swim away if you hadn't locked her up."

I have to stifle a laugh at that and Octo sighs heavily.

Finally, I say, "I won't try to swim away. I wouldn't even know where to go. And I don't want to be trapped by humans, so I wouldn't try to go back to the beach."

Octo seems to relax at that.

Ovaggd'tho gestures to the cage and adds, "Why do you even have this?"

"I found it and thought it might come in handy one day for something." Octo replies, a little bit defensively.

Ovaggd'tho snorts. "Like trapping your mate." Then he roars again with laughter.

Octo hangs his head in shame, and Ovaggd'tho claps him on the back again. "Come on, Octhogh'xu, you know I'll tease you about this mess for a long time."

Octo just nods. "I know, I deserve that."

Xaiolpa interrupts their teasing. "How about we go to our cave? I'm assuming Naomi hasn't gotten out to see much." She side-eyes Octo. "We can gather food on the way, and Naomi will be able to see our world and learn a valuable skill."

I give her a huge smile. "I think that would be amazing." I look to Octo to see his reaction. He seems tense, but he nods in agreement.

Ovaggd'tho and Xaiolpa swim out through the window first, then Octo follows. Once he's through the window, he stops and holds a hand out for me to come through. I take his hand and swim out of the ship for the first time.

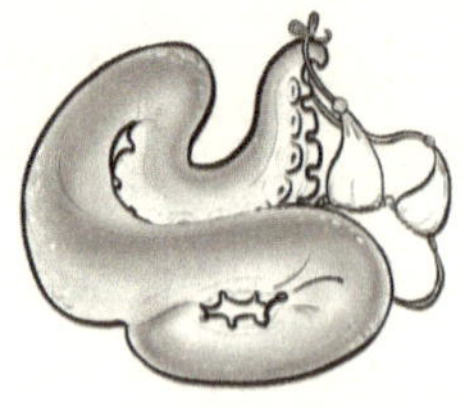

Chapter 14

Naomi

I'm instantly amazed. The inside of the ship was dull and boring to look at, especially since I'd spent so much time trapped there with nothing to do.

But outside...it's full of life and beauty. There are silky, sandy spots where crabs and other crustaceans skitter around, stirring up little puffs of sand everywhere they go. There are large rocky areas with fans of bristly red corals, spiny branches of pale pink and purple corals, and masses of squiggly yellow corals that look like brains growing all over them. Pale pink clumps of anemone tentacles reach out from the nooks and crannies of all the coral, and little clownfish peek out from the safety of their venomous homes.

Brightly colored fish swim everywhere. There are flashes of yellow or blue or orange or even teal as fish swim by. Some fish swim in schools, and some dart in and out of coral by themselves. A school of small blue fish swims by us. As I watch them, a large translucent blue jellyfish casually float above my head. I gasp as I take it all in.

I turn back to look at the outside of the ship and it's sitting on the bottom of the ocean, its waterlogged wood resting on the pale sand. The back half of the ship is buried in a huge kelp forest. Fish dart around and between the long green strands of kelp. I watch as a sleek gray seal twists and dives gracefully in and out of the forest. It stops to watch us for a moment, then dives back in between the strands.

I turn to look at Octo. "Can we go in there?"

He smiles and nods. "If that's what you would like."

I give him a huge radiant smile and nod excitedly. Then I dart off toward the kelp forest so much faster than I thought I could. I stop as soon as I get to the first strands of kelp. Octo catches up with me, looking worried.

I laugh, "Sorry, I didn't realize how fast I could swim now."

He has a smile of relief when I say that. "I thought maybe you were trying to run from me."

I notice over his shoulder that Ovaggd'tho and Xaiolpa are still floating where we just came from. "Oh, they're waiting for us." I glance toward the kelp, then I look to Octo. "I guess we should go. Can we come back here later?"

"Don't worry, they don't mind waiting a little bit." he reassures me.

Worried, I ask, "Are you sure?"

He nods. Then, I excitedly swim into the kelp. Octo follows me in. I twist and swim between the strands. Once I'm in the middle of it, I look up in wonder at the sunlight streaming through the water. I hold on to a strand of kelp and float there on my back for a few moments, just looking at it. As I twist to flip over, a bright color on the ocean floor catches my attention, and I dive down to the bottom and find a giant starfish. It's large and orange and spiny and has a lot of arms, so many more than most starfish. There are also a handful of purple urchins slowly crawling their way along the ocean floor.

I feel the water move behind me and turn to see that the seal is back. It's swimming around me as if it's trying to figure out what I am. With a huge smile, I hold a hand out. It swims close enough to barely bump its nose against my palm, then darts off again to hide in the kelp. I look above me, and Octo is floating nearby watching me with a smile on his face.

I swim up to him. "This is so beautiful! Thank you for letting me see it."

He nods.

I say, "I don't want to keep them waiting any longer though, we should go."

When I turn to swim out of the kelp forest, I realize that I have gotten myself completely turned around and I have no idea which way is out.

Octo must notice that I'm looking around like I'm lost. He takes my hand and swims me in the correct direction to get out.

Once we are out of the forest, we swim straight toward Ovaggd'tho and Xaiolpa. When we are close enough for them to hear, I say, "Sorry for making you wait."

I feel ridiculous, like a child.

Xaiolpa waves a hand dismissively. "Don't worry, Naomi. This is your first time out exploring, of course you want to see everything." She gives Octo a pointed look.

Ovaggd'tho and Xaiolpa begin swimming toward their home, and Octo and I follow.

Along the way I keep my eyes glued to the ocean floor, looking at everything. There's so much coral, and so much sea life.

Eventually, Octo grabs my hand so that I stop swimming. I look up and watch as Xaiolpa dives down to the ocean floor. She grabs something and hands it to Ovaggd'tho and he puts it in a netted bag like the one Octo carries.

When I look over at Octo, he's pulling out his bag too. Then he says, "Come, I'll show you where to find oysters."

I follow him as he dives down to a rocky area at the ocean floor. I watch as he breaks oysters off of different rocks and puts them in the bag. He points to some. "Here, you try."

I look at the oysters attached to the rock and give him a wary look. I'm pretty sure humans usually have to use some sort of tool to do this, so I really don't think I'm going to be strong enough to. He makes a circular motion with his hand, telling me to go on. I grab one and break it off the rock easily, then I hand it to him. As he puts it in the bag, I say, "I don't think I would have been able to do that before. Am I stronger now?"

He shrugs. "Probably."

We continue harvesting oysters for a few more minutes, then he motions for me to follow him. He takes me away from the rocks to a sandier area and shows me how to catch crabs. We hunt for those, and once our bag is full, we swim over to Ovaggd'tho and Xaiolpa.

Xaiolpa says, "We are almost to our cave. Come, we can show you where we live so you know how close we are if you ever need anything. Then we can enjoy our dinner."

They swim off and we follow them.

Once we get to their cave, we enjoy the food we caught. I'm completely famished and eat so much. I notice Octo giving me appreciative looks as I eat. As I'm eating, I look over at Ovaggd'tho's and Xaiolpa's net. I notice that they have wiggling fish and other crustaceans mixed in with the crabs in their net. I watch as Xaiolpa pulls a pretty yellow fish out of the net. The fish isn't moving, so it must already be dead.

I lean closer to look, and Xaiolpa notices. "Would you like to try it, Naomi?"

"Oh...no, I don't want to take your food. I just haven't eaten any of the fish down here. How did you catch it?" I ask.

She laughs, "You just grab them. Once you have one, you sink your claws into their side to kill them."

I raise my eyebrows. "You just grab them; aren't they fast?"

She gives me a soft smile. "At first they are, but with enough practice, you eventually learn to read their movements, then it's easy."

I look at the fish in her hand. "But how do you eat it?" I don't understand how she's going to clean and gut it underwater.

She smiles then using her sharp claws, she grabs the fish by the gills and rips the entrails out and tosses them to the side. Then she lifts it up to her mouth and bites off the tail end of the fish.

I stare at her in shock. "You just yank the guts out and then eat everything else...even the bones?"

She just nods.

I watch as several small fish swim up to the discarded entrails and begin picking at it.

Octo has been watching our conversation, and he says, "We can catch some fish for you if you would like."

I give him a wide-eyed look. "I've never eaten a fish like that...bones and scales and all."

Xaiolpa adds, "They are good, you will like them." She reaches into her net and tries to hand me another fish. I look over at Octo and he has an unhappy look. I think he doesn't like the idea of someone else feeding me. And I'm not sure how I feel about just ripping the insides of a fish out with my bare hands. I've always been more of a girly girl. Fishing and hunting were never my things.

I say, "Thank you. I think I'll stick to crab right now. I will have to work up my courage to try eating a fish like that."

She smiles then takes a big bite out of the fish while I stare at her.

They all fall into a quiet conversation and are enjoying each other's company, but I'm too distracted to pay attention. I can't stop looking at all the beauty around me.

They have a beautiful mound of bright red coral near the entrance to their cave. Little yellow fish swim around and explore it, while a few small red and white shrimp crawl around picking up specks of something to eat. There are several pale pink anemones tucked away in the safety of the coral. Each anemone has at least one tiny clown fish swimming around it and darting through its tentacles.

Movement draws my attention away from the clown fish, and I look down just in time to see a couple of small, speckled sting rays skate by just above the sand.

Eventually the food is gone, and everyone is done talking. Octo brushes my cheek to draw my attention to him. Then he says, "Naomi, it's going to be dark soon. We should go back to our nest."

I nod my head. I thank Xaiolpa and Ovaggd'tho for their hospitality. Xaiolpa swims over to me and says, "Tomorrow, when Octhogh'xu and Ovaggd'tho go out patrolling their territories, I'll come to your home so that you don't need to go back in that cage."

I smile. "That would be wonderful."

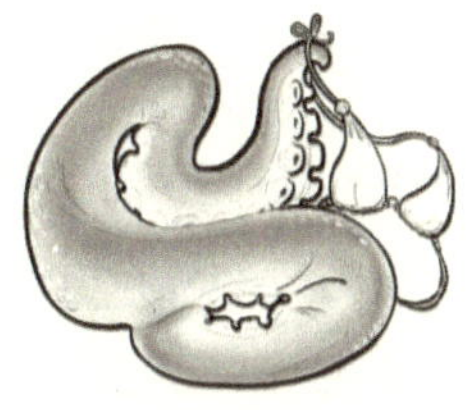

Chapter 15

Both Octo and I are quiet as we swim back to the ship. I'm too busy watching everything and looking everywhere to hold a conversation.

As we get near the ship, I notice a shadow of something large swimming near it. I gasp when I realize it's a shark.

I grab onto Octo's arm. "It's a shark!"

He looks at it and chuckles. "Come, this will be a good opportunity to teach you."

"Are you crazy?! That's a big shark!" I try to swim backwards, but he pulls me forward by my arm. "You said we would practice with a small shark!"

He chuckles again, "That is not a big shark. Come, it will be fine, these types don't usually try to bite anyway."

"What do you mean that's not a big shark?! That's a big fucking shark! And hold on a minute—*usually*...they don't *usually* bite?!"

I'm still trying to swim in the opposite direction, so he wraps his arm around my waist and slides me onto his shoulder. "Come, it will be fine. And trust me, a big shark is much bigger than that."

"What?!"

Octo just chuckles at me again.

As we get near the shark, he takes me off his shoulder and keeps me in front of him with his arm still around my waist.

The shark is swimming in large circles looking for something, probably food...or a person to eat.

Octo calmly explains, "In a minute, it will probably come over here to inspect us." I whimper, but Octo continues, "If it tries to bump you, just push it down by its snout. It will swim away from you."

The shark begins tightening its circular path around us. Before I know it, I'm looking at the shark as it swims directly at us. I press myself against Octo's body. I'm so afraid that I can hear the blood pounding in my ears. Octo grabs my hand and pushes my arm out with his. Together, we push the shark's nose down and it swims right by us without doing anything.

I let out a sigh of relief and laugh, then watch as the shark swims away.

Octo still has his arm around my waist, and I'm still pressed against him. In my ear, he quietly says, "Good, Naomi, you did well." I turn my head to look at him, and only then realize how close we are. We are practically nose to nose looking at each other.

We stay frozen like that for a few breaths, then Octo says, "Let's go to our nest."

Then we swim through the broken window and into the ship.

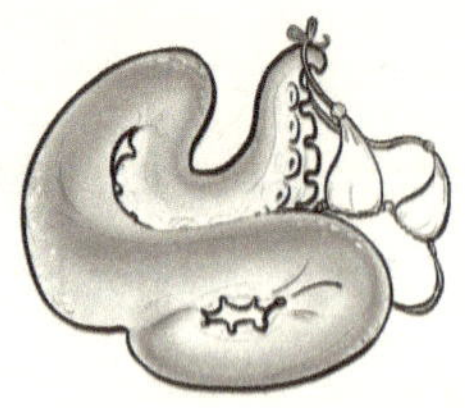

Chapter 16

It's beginning to get dark now, and Octo goes to the nest to sleep. I swim over with him, then I pause for a moment.

"Um…Octo…I need to…uh…relieve myself."

He looks at me curiously and says, "Okay."

"Um…where can I go?"

He raises his eyebrows at me.

"Humans usually have a bathroom that we go to when we need to relieve ourselves."

He gives me a confused look and says, "You're shy of these things? What did you do while you were in the cage?"

"I had to just…you know…go. I couldn't go anywhere else because *someone* wouldn't let me out, but now I would like somewhere to relieve myself…in private."

He scoffs. "You don't need some place private. Those of us that live underwater are not concerned about that."

I press my palms into my eyes, take a deep breath, and pray to the gods for patience. Then I calmly say, "I'm glad you are comfortable with that, but I'm not yet. Is there somewhere that I can go?"

He sighs and points toward where the door to the cabin would have been. "If you swim in there, there are other chambers that you can use for privacy."

"Thank you, Octo."

I quickly swim through the door and into what was probably a short hallway. There is another doorway immediately to my left and I go in. It's a small room, but it will work. I look around, but it's not like I'm going to find a toilet. A toilet wouldn't even work in this situation. This has to be the weirdest bathroom situation I've ever been in.

There is some stuff piled in the corner, and I realize that there is a bucket in that pile. Oh, my gods, a bucket! I can work with that.

I look around realizing that I need to figure out something for toilet paper. This room has a small window that is broken out, and I can see some of the kelp from the forest floating just outside. I reach through the window and tear off some pieces. I grab the bucket and place it in the corner and strip off my swimsuit bottoms. Once I'm done, I throw the used kelp out the window and empty the bucket out the window too. I'm just going to trust that everything floats away.

I put my bucket back down in the corner and put a couple of heavier things on top of it, then I put my swimsuit bottoms back on.

Well, that was weird.

As I leave my new restroom, I look down the hallway to the rest of the ship.

There's a closed door at the end of the hall. That door would lead out to the rest of the ship. I look back toward the doorway leading back to Octo. I really want to see what the rest of the ship looks like. I try to gauge how long I've been gone, and I decide that I think I have enough time to do a little bit of exploring before Octo gets worried.

The door, along with various other patches of wall throughout the ship, is crusted over in patches of barnacles. As I get closer to the door, I study the little barnacles. I can see their little fan-like filaments fluttering out of the shells. I reach out to touch one and it quickly disappears back into the shell.

I look at the door again. The knob is stuck from years of being in salt water. I try to jiggle it, but it's pointless. There is no amount of wiggling that will unstick it.

I push against the door, and after leaning my shoulder into it, it breaks free of whatever has been keeping it closed—probably more barnacles. I open it enough to swim through and discover an amazing little world of sea life.

The first thing I notice once I get the door open is that the back half of the ship isn't buried in the kelp like I thought—it's just gone. It's like the ship was broken in half, and the back half is gone.

The kelp begins about ten feet away from the door. Little crabs scuttle away from me and disappear into the kelp. Several colorful fish also dart away. There are clumps of purple urchins slowly making their way along the sand toward the kelp forest.

Looking around, I see that there are broken pieces of wood and wreckage strewn about and half buried in the sand. These pieces of the ship might once have been from the land, but the sea has claimed them now. Hard barnacles grow all over them. Little red shrimp and small colorful fish pick their way over these clusters. I watch as a small blue and yellow fish pecks at the feather-like ends that poke out of a barnacle. There are even a few pale pink anemones clinging to the clumps, with little orange clownfish residents.

It's beautiful. I look for another minute or two before I decide I need to go back inside. I don't want Octo to think I've run off.

I swim back in, and pull the door closed. There's no way to actually latch it, so I just pull it as closed as I can get it. Once I'm satisfied that it won't just swing open, I turn around and head back up the hallway.

When I swim back into Octo's room. He's waiting for me in the nest, and he gives me a curious look as I come in.

I just smile because I have no idea what to even say. I'm pretty sure you don't impress guys by saying 'Thanks for letting me find a bucket to take a crap in'.

That thought catches me off guard. Am I trying to impress him?

Finally, I say, "Can I come sleep over there so I don't float away?"

Octo nods. He looks a little nervous. I notice some of his tentacles are coiling around each other. I swim over to him, and he coils his tentacles around me like he did last night. I nuzzle my face into one, and say, "Thank you, Octo, I had a nice day today."

He reaches a hand down and strokes my hair. "You're welcome, Naomi."

I lay there, facing him as his coils hold me close to him. He continues stroking my hair, then eventually his hand moves down to my neck, and I feel his knuckles lightly brush my skin. I shiver at the light touch, then I nuzzle my face into his tentacle more. He runs his knuckles down my neck and onto my shoulder.

I look at one of the tentacles nearest me and begin exploring it with my fingers. I stroke a finger along it, trying to figure out where it's sensitive. I rub my thumb against one of the suckers. Octo shivers at that touch. Gods, the suckers are sensitive. My mind immediately goes to all the places those could be used, and heat pools in my groin.

My feelings are at war with each other. Why do I keep getting turned on by him? Even though he kidnapped me, I'm drawn to him. Is it the mating bond? Is it that he's being nice to me? He let me out of my cage. Or is this actually Stockholm Syndrome?

I finally decide that I just need to stop thinking and let it be what it is. I continue rubbing my thumb over one sucker after another enjoying the feeling of Octo shivering from my touch.

Before too long, Octo fists his fingers in my hair and lightly pulls my head up toward him.

I can see the lust in his eye. His voice is thick and husky when he says, "Naomi...do you know what you do?"

I reach my hand forward and run my fingers over his chest and onto his stomach. Then I say, "Yes."

I see another shiver run through him.

I pull myself toward him and press my lips against his. It startles him and he pulls his face back from mine.

"Naomi...what..."

"It's a kiss. Humans do this to show affection to their mate." I don't give him time to respond, I just press my lips to his again.

He doesn't pull away this time. He presses his lips against mine. His mouth isn't the same as mine, but we still fit together. I slightly brush my tongue against his lips, and I feel him jolt in surprise, but then he relaxes and opens his mouth to me. His teeth are sharp—well my teeth are sharp now too—so I very carefully slide my tongue into his mouth.

He brushes his tongue against mine. It's thicker than mine and slick. As we continue to kiss, he wraps his arms around me and pulls me closer so I'm in his lap, and I wrap my arms around his neck. I begin to feel his tentacles coil around me. One snakes around my thigh as another wraps around my ankle. Yet another one slides over my hip and hooks around my waist. The longer we kiss, the more comfortable he becomes with it. He takes control of it, and his larger tongue delves into my mouth.

Eventually, I break away from our kiss and begin kissing and nibbling down his neck. He groans as I do this, and his groan sends a shiver through me. A bolt of longing shoots straight to my groin.

"Octo...I need you, please touch me."

He begins kissing my neck. He brushes his tongue over my gills, and I shiver. He whispers, "Show me what you need me to do."

I pause to look at him. "You've never..."

He chuckles and continues kissing down my neck. "You are human."

Oh, right. Of course he wouldn't know how to please a human.

He stops kissing me and says, "But also, no, I haven't mated with any females. I was waiting until I scented the mate that I would give my mating bite to. I tried once when I was younger...it didn't end well." He rubs the scars where his missing eye would be.

"Oh, my gods, she did that to you?" I'm horrified.

He sighs, "I was young. I'd just come of age, and my father was still alive, so I hadn't battled for my territory yet. I scented her and thought maybe she could be my mate. I ambushed her and she fought me. It's a female's right to fight their potential mates to ensure that their mate is strong and worthy of them. I did not win the fight."

I don't know what to say. "That's terrible, Octo. I'm sorry that happened."

"After that, I vowed to be the strongest and most worthy so that I could claim my mate when I found her. I did not pursue any other females. I waited until I scented you."

I kiss him again. "I'm sorry you went through that, Octo."

"It's as it should be. Now I've found you, and I know that you're the perfect mate for me." Then with a small growl, he says, "Now, female, show me how to please you."

I smile as I press another kiss to his mouth, then I reach behind me, unhook my bikini top, and slip it off. "Let's start here."

Instantly, one of his tentacles slides up and cups one of my breasts. He lightly palms his hand around the other one. As gently as he can with his claws, he rolls my nipple between his fingers. I gasp at that small touch.

He watches my face and asks, "Is that sensitive?"

I whimper and nod as he continues to roll my nipple in his fingers. Then he brushes a sucker over the other nipple, causing my breath to hitch.

He leans down and sucks my nipple into his mouth. I feel his tongue brush against it. The sucker still gently massages my other nipple. I moan as he licks and sucks on it.

Huskily he says, "Tell me more, Naomi, tell me what else pleases you."

I reach down and slip my bikini bottoms off.

He groans, and I see him take a deep breath in.

I slide my hand down to my pussy and press my fingers through my folds, feeling how slick I am. "Here."

Because of his claws, he gently touches me. He brushes his fingers through my pubic hair, then gives me a curious look. As he continues to toy with my pubic hair, he says, "I did not know that humans have hair here."

I nod. All I can focus on is his hand and how it's delicately brushing against me. It feels like agony waiting for him to touch me—to really touch me, and I whimper. "Octo...please."

He gives me what I'm begging for. He very gently slides his knuckle through my pussy. I gasp as he lightly grazes my clit.

"This part is sensitive?" He brushes his knuckle over my clit again.

I'm breathless as I say, "Yes, that's the most sensitive part."

He growls deep in his throat as he brushes it again, and I moan.

"There's more though." I guide his hand back toward my entrance and press against it, so his knuckle dips into me. "This is where your cock goes."

He lets out a low groan. Then one of his tentacles slides toward my pussy. He moves his hand as it slips through my folds and presses into my core. I moan, "Oh fuck, Octo," as his tentacle delves into me.

I wrap my arms around his neck and cling to him as he continues to press into me. It feels like it's getting thicker inside me, so he must be coiling it on itself, or knotting it up, or something. Then Octo brushes his knuckle against my clit again, and I moan loudly.

He murmurs into my ear, "You said this is the most sensitive part, so does it feel best if I do this while I fuck you?"

Between moans I manage to say, "Yes."

I feel another tentacle slip into me. They thrust in and out of me, fucking me while he rubs my clit. I bury my face into his shoulder and writhe in his coils. I feel others wrapping around my leg and thigh, holding me in place.

I feel my legs start to tremble as my pleasure builds inside me. I moan into his neck, "Don't stop, oh gods, don't stop." His groan is so deep, it sounds more like a growl, and it vibrates his chest.

I feel a third tentacle thrust into me with the other two, and I cry out. I'm so close to coming. They thrust into me harder and faster, and then he brushes a second knuckle over my clit, and it pushes me over the edge and my orgasm crashes through me. I scream as I come. My pussy clenches around his tentacles, and my body spasms in his grip.

Once my muscles finally relax, Octo kisses me and then gives me a knowing grin. "Did I please my mate?"

I'm still breathless, but I say, "Yes. Gods yes." Then I kiss him deeply. "But you aren't done yet. I still want your cock inside me."

He groans into my neck. "My mate is so demanding."

I chuckle, "Careful or I'll bite you again." Then I gently nip at his neck, and he lets out a guttural groan. "Mmm, it sounds like you want that." I nip harder, and he groans again. I feel all of his muscles tighten like he's restraining himself, but I don't want him restraining himself.

I kiss his neck, then murmur, "Fuck me, Octhogh'xu."

This time he actually does growl. "I like it when my mate actually says my name correctly."

Huskily I say, "Do a good job, and maybe I'll say it correctly again."

He spins me around so I'm facing away from him. A tentacle wraps around each of my thighs spreading my legs wide and holding them open. I feel others sliding up my back. One wraps around me just under my breasts and another one slides up to gently wrap around my throat.

Then I feel his cock nudge against my entrance, and I gasp. He grips my hips with his claws, then he slowly starts pressing into me. His cock very quickly tapers to be thick, thicker than I'm used to. I moan and gasp as he presses all the way into me. "Fuck, Octo. Gods, it's so thick."

He groans, and I feel one of his tentacles slip up to my pussy. I gasp as it slides over my clit, then I feel a sucker latch onto my clit, and I let out a loud cry. "Fuck!"

He pulls back, then quickly thrusts back into me. His thrusts are fast and hard, and the sucker works magic on my clit. I come apart quickly. My pussy pulses around his cock as I come, and he groans as he thrusts into me one last time. He lets out a deep growl as he comes, filling me with his seed.

Once the aftershocks of our orgasms have finished working through us, he gently loosens his grip on me and then turns me so he can tuck me into his side. He wraps his tentacles around me.

He leans down and kisses me deeply, then I snuggle against him and fall asleep.

Chapter 17

OCTHOGH'XU / OCTO

My mate is sated and sleeps peacefully in my tentacles. The Gods of the Sea have smiled on me. Naomi is my perfect mate. Yes, she's feisty, and fights me on nearly everything, but I wouldn't have her any other way. She's the greatest gift I have ever been given.

I curl up next to her and shut my eye to get some rest too.

***

The next morning, I wake before Naomi does. I curl around her and watch her as she sleeps. Today I'm going to leave her with Xaiolpa while I patrol my territory and check on the human situation on that beach. I'm terribly anxious about this. I'm still afraid she will run off. I think back to our mating last night, and how eager she was for me. Certainly, she will want to stay after that.

Naomi wakes as I lay there fretting about leaving her. She stretches and yawns, then cuddles her face into my neck.

"Good morning, Octo."

I reply, "Good morning, my mate. Did you sleep well?"

Her reply is a muffled, "Mmhmmm."

I play with her hair as it floats around her head.

After a few minutes, Naomi wiggles up to my face and kisses me. Her kisses surprised me yesterday. My people don't do anything like that, and now I wonder why. I enjoy kissing my mate. I deepen our kiss and slide my tongue into her mouth. We continue kissing like that until she makes a little whimpering noise and pulls back.

Breathlessly she says, "Do you have to leave soon?"

I shrug. "Not urgently. I don't want to leave until Xaiol-pa gets here."

She breathes a sigh, "Good. I want to try something."

"Try what?" I ask.

"I'll show you." Then she begins kissing down my neck and onto my chest She makes her way down to my stom-ach.

My cock is hard and aching. I groan, "Naomi."

She just gives me a knowing smile, then she reaches through my tentacles and wraps her hand around my cock. She strokes it, and I moan.

She giggles, then completely surprises me by sliding down and licking up the length of my cock and circling the tip of it with her tongue. Waves of pleasure roll through me.

I groan loudly. "Naomi..."

Before I can say anything else, she licks it again, then sucks it into her mouth.

I gasp as I watch it disappear in her mouth. She sucks in as much of it as she can. She wraps her hand around what she can't fit. She's watching my face, watching my reactions, and I moan as I watch her work my cock.

My tentacles coil on each other and wrap around her. One of them wraps up her thigh and slides into her heat. She moans around my cock, and it feels so good that I growl.

I work another one into her heat, causing her to moan more. I love the little sounds that she makes as I give her pleasure. I latch one of my suckers onto that sensitive nub at the apex of her sex, and she cries out around my cock. Her cry entices me to give her more. I fuck her with my tentacles as she sucks on me. Both of us moan as we work each other into a frenzy.

All of her moaning is sending vibrations through my cock, and I feel like I will come at any second. Gasping I say, "Naomi...I..."

With my cock still in her mouth, she hums, "Hmmm?"

I groan again. "If you...keep...that..." I gasp. "I will..." I break off into another moan before I can finish the sentence.

She chuckles around my cock and hums again, "Mmh-mmm."

My head lolls back and I gasp as the vibrations of her voice send me right to the edge.

She seems determined to make me come with her mouth, and I groan as I try desperately to hold myself still so I don't thrust into her mouth and hurt her. But I won't be outdone; I'll make her come too. I thrust my tentacles inside her faster and frantically work all of my suckers hoping that the one latched on her sensitive nub will work harder.

With that, she practically screams then cries frantically around my cock and I feel her body spasm as her sex grips my tentacles.

The extra vibrations push me over the edge, and I yell as I come. Then I watch as her throat works and swallows down all my seed.

She pulls her mouth off of my cock then licks up the length of it one last time, and I shudder. She giggles as she slides back up my body. I carefully cup her jaw with my hand and pull her toward my face for a kiss.

After we kiss, she sighs as she nuzzles back into my side. After a few minutes, she says, "I wish we could stay like this all day."

"I do too. But I must at least check on the humans at the beach."

That catches her attention. "The beach that you took me from?"

I nod.

She furrows her brow. "Are there a lot of humans there?"

"Yes, more than usual."

"Is it because of me?"

I pause. Part of me is still worried that she will go back to them the first chance she gets.

She gives me an impatient look. "Just tell me. Trust me, I'm not going back. I don't want to be locked away in some lab and poked and prodded for the rest of my life."

I sigh and say, "Yes, I believe it is because of you."

She gives me a worried look. "Octo, it's a big deal for a human woman to go missing from a beach like that. Please be careful. They'll be looking for any clue of where I am. Please don't get too close."

"I'll be safe. I have a reason to come home now."

She smiles softly and kisses me.

Just then I hear a female voice at the entrance to our home. "Hello? Octhogh'xu...Naomi? It's Xaiolpa. I stopped by a few minutes ago, but you two were...ah...busy, so I left and now I'm back."

Naomi gasps next to me and whispers, "Oh my gods, did she see us?"

I laugh. "Don't worry Naomi. My people are not shy about such things." Then I say, "Hello, Xaiolpa, we're here."

We both swim out of our home to meet Xaiolpa. I pick up my spear on the way out. Once we are outside, I notice that Naomi looks nervous and shy. Is she embarrassed that Xaiolpa saw us? Then I realize that she's holding her arm over her breasts in an attempt to block them from sight, and I remember the clothing she removed before we mated.

I say, "Xaiolpa, may I have a moment with my mate?"

"Of course, I'll just swim over to the kelp and look for good strands for today. Take your time." Then she swims off to the kelp forest.

I look to Naomi. "Are you well Naomi? Are you worried about Xaiolpa seeing us?"

She furrows her brow. "Yes! But...I'm also...well I was so surprised that she saw us that I wasn't thinking when I swam out here, and I'm not wearing my swimsuit." She pauses for a minute. "I don't know how I forgot something as important as clothes. It just felt natural to swim out here without it. None of you wear clothing, but humans cover their bodies. What am I supposed to do? I'm half fish and half human."

"You're not half fish, you are you. You're what you're supposed to be in order to be my mate. You don't need to wear clothing here. No one will think anything of it," I reassure her.

She gives me another worried look. "But my boobs are huge—and everyone can see everything. And I look so different than everyone else." She gestures to her body as she says this.

"No one will think anything of it," I repeat as I shake my head. "It's just the way your body is." Something occurs to me and I stop to think for a second. "Actually, they'll probably think it's odd if you continue to wear clothing while living here."

That seems to put her at ease a little. "Really?"

"Yes. You're fine, don't worry. Plus, I want all of my people to see how beautiful my mate is." I give her a kiss. "Swim over to Xaiolpa and do whatever she tells you to today. Don't argue with her. Please be careful, my Naomi."

She rolls her eyes at me then gives me another kiss. "Okay, okay. I will. You be careful too. Remember what I said."

"I will."

I watch as she swims to Xaiolpa. Once she gets there, she turns to look back at me, and I wave before I swim off toward the beach.

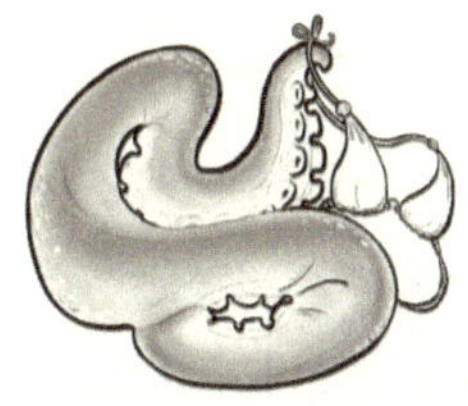

Chapter 18

Naomi

Once I get to Xaiolpa, I wave to Octo and watch as he swims away. Then I turn to her and say, "So, what are we doing today?"

She gives me a bright-eyed look and says, "I thought we could harvest some kelp, and I'll show you how to make a net for gathering food."

I get excited by that. "That's a great idea! I want one of my own so that I can help Octo... Octhogh'xu."

She nods, then she gives me a conspiratorial look. "I have to ask; you had your mouth on his cock when I first came by. Is that something all humans do?"

Oh my gods. I cover my face with my hands as it heats up. My face feels so hot that I swear it could boil water.

Xaiolpa quickly says, "Oh no, Naomi, don't be embarrassed. Our people aren't shy about mating." She pauses for a moment, then says, "I only ask because I have never heard of that before. Our people don't use our mouths, but it certainly seemed...exciting."

Oh my gods. I take a deep breath, then laugh nervously, and quickly say, "Yes, humans use their mouths for all sorts of things. We kiss each other. Females use their mouths on their mates, and males also use their mouths on their mates."

She gives me a surprised look. "Males use their mouths on their mates too?"

The rest of the day was spent laughing easily and trading sex tips while we harvested kelp and made nets out of it. She wanted to know about blow jobs, so I explained to her how to give one. I also explained to her how a mate can use their mouth on female...well...human female anatomy. She described what females of her kind have, and it sounded very similar to a human vagina. Instead of a clit, they have three sucker type things that are sensitive and give them orgasms. She said they're like suckers, but not suckers.

Three clits—that doesn't sound like a bad deal to me. I'm a little jealous now, actually. Too bad Octo's mating bite didn't give me that.

***

Octhogh'xu / Octo

I swim to the beach to check on the humans. There are still too many of them. And now there seems to be more going into the water. This can't be good.

I watch them from a safe place hidden in the reef, but I see them looking at the reef more and more. They come out in their machine boats, and the swimmers jump into the water. These machine boats and swimmers look different than the ones that were here the other day. These boats seem to have more things on them. The swimmers carry a lot of things with them underwater, and I fear that they are weapons. They swim right up to the reef, then they float there, studying it. They seem to be watching for something, and I'm worried that something is me. I think back to the day that the one must have seen me. I was distracted and careless. I think he saw me swim from the tunnel to the reef.

I check on the tunnel, and as I watch, I see swimmers go into the tunnel. I groan. They are hunting me. My territory is safe as long as they don't try to cross the border. Once they start to cross, I'll be forced to defend it. And there are too many of them. If I'm called to fight them, I will fall.

I feel like I ought to call for aid from the others, but I don't want to. It would mean many hours out here with other Guardians. We would have to set up a watch rotation to keep an eye on the humans. Instead, I want to be home coiled around my mate. I want to kiss her and bury my cock inside her.

As I think about the way it felt to fuck her, I make up my mind. I'll go to Ovaggd'tho before I go home and consult with him on this. Then I'll go home to my Naomi, and I'll check on the humans again tomorrow.

I begin swimming for home. I swim past my nest and continue on to Ovaggd'tho's territory. I use his scent to find him.

Once I see him, I wave, then I quickly swim to his side.

He seems startled to see me. "What is it Octhogh'xu? Are the females well?"

"Yes, They're fine. I need your opinion on something within my territory."

I explain the beach and the humans and how there are progressively more of them, and that I think one saw me. I sigh, "It seems as though they're interested in the reef now. I fear they'll begin to cross over into my territory. There are too many for me to fight. It's because of Naomi. She cautioned me that it's a big deal for a female to go missing like she did. I think they'll not give up their search for her easily."

He's frowning by this point. "None of them have crossed yet?"

I shake my head.

He looks out to the ocean. "Night will come soon. Humans don't like to be out in the water at night, so I think it will be safe until tomorrow. Tomorrow, we will rise early and watch the beach together. We may need to call for aid."

I nod solemnly.

He clasps me on the shoulder. "Go home to your mate and enjoy her company tonight."

I smile, flashes of memories from last night and this morning running through my head. "I'll send your mate home to you as soon as I get home."

He nods a thank you, and I swim off.

I gather crabs and oysters on the way for our dinner. I decide to add a few urchins to the bag as well. Naomi has not tried those yet and may enjoy them.

When I arrive home, I find Naomi and Xaiolpa still by the kelp field. They've been working on nets while I was gone, and Naomi's is coming along nicely.

She smiles and shows it to me when I swim up. Pride swells in my chest at the way she's embracing our life. I kiss her deeply, not caring that Xaiolpa is still there.

After the kiss, she says, "How was your day? How was the beach?"

My mood darkens. "Not good."

She gives me a quick worried look. "Did something happen?"

I shake my head. "No, but now there are more humans, and they are looking at the reef with interest. I fear it's just a matter of time before they try to cross into my territory." I look to Xaiolpa. "I went to your territory and spoke with your mate. He's going with me to the beach tomorrow to help me watch it. We will decide from there if we need to call for aid."

Xaiolpa absently reaches up and clasps her hand around her necklace, then she nods. "We will handle whatever the humans decide to do."

I notice Naomi watching both of us closely with a look of concern on her face.

I nod in agreement with Xaiolpa, then I say, "I told Ovaggd'tho that I would send you home to him when I got here. Thank you for staying with Naomi, and for helping to teach her valuable skills for living in our world."

She gives Naomi a knowing grin then says, "Oh, Naomi isn't the only one that's learned new things today. I think Ovaggd'tho will be very pleased to see me this evening."

Then she swims off and waves back to us before she gets out of sight.

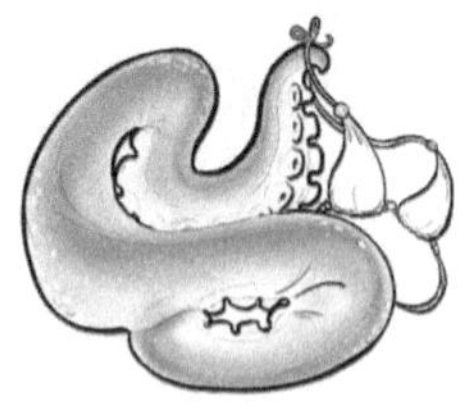

Chapter 19

Naomi

I watch Xaiolpa swim off and then look back at Octo.

He gives me a curious look and says, "What did that mean?"

I laugh nervously, "Oh...well...she saw us this morning and wanted to know how to use her mouth on her mate. I explained it to her."

Octo reaches over and runs his thumb against my lip, then says, "I imagine he's going to be very pleased this evening then." He reaches down, embraces me, and gives me another kiss. Who knew Octo could be this affectionate?

As we gather up my net supplies and swim into our home, I ask, "Hey, so what was all of that about the beach and the humans?"

Octo sighs, "The humans haven't stopped looking for you. And I was careless the other day, I think one of them saw me."

My eyes go wide. "That's not good."

"No, it's not good. Now there are more humans, but these humans are different. These come out in machine boats and bring tools underwater. Many of them are looking at the reef."

Fear flares through me. "Octo, you can't go near those humans. Please."

He puts his hand against my cheek. "I won't."

"What happens if they cross the reef? What do Guardians do? I don't understand any of this."

Octo sets down our things, then his bag of food. He digs in the bag and hands me a crab. "Naomi, eat and I'll explain."

I nod and take a bite.

He looks at me and asks, "Do you know anything of Guardians?"

I shake my head. "Just the mating bite part. And you have territory."

He pulls out a crab and takes a bite out of it, then says, "The people in this realm are mostly divided into Elven and Guardians, but for now, I'll just tell you about Guardians. There are Guardians on land and in the water, and I'm told even in the sky. Ovaggd'tho, Xaiolpa, and I are one type of Sea Guardian. There are many different types of Sea Guardians, and they have many different purposes. My people are known to be fierce fighters, so we are frequently rewarded with territory to protect." He cracks open an oyster and swallows it, then continues. "Not all Sea Guardians look like me, there are many different ways they can look; some look like fish or crabs or eels, some look more like coral. There are even some that have the ability to change shape and can change into water itself. Those are the most powerful because they have more magic than the rest of us. They are even able to control the way water flows."

I interrupt, "Do you have magic?"

He shakes his head. "No. I have to use my strength and skill to defend my territory."

He cracks open an oyster and hands it to me, and I ask, "But what about the mating bite, that's magic, right?"

He bites into another crab. "Yes, but that's different. That's magic that affects all Guardians. When we find our mate, we are compelled to bite them, and the magic here, in this world, binds us together. There are other similar magical things that have effects on me. After I won my territory, we had a ceremony that magically bound me to my territory. Now I can sense intruders when they cross into my territory. I'm also compelled to fight if intruders enter my territory. They say that is part of the magical binding, but I just feel it is my duty."

I take another crab from Octo, and chew on it thoughtfully. "Who did the magic to bind you to your territory?"

"One of the Guardians, the type that can change into water. He performs all of the binding ceremonies in our part of the sea."

Octo hands me another crab, and I pull off a leg while I absorb all of this. "So, what's special about the reef?"

"It's the border between this world and the human world."

That makes me think about the beach. "So, the beach that you took me from, that was part of the human world, right?"

He nods.

"But—I don't understand. Where are we? You say this world and the human world. What does that mean?"

Octo looks at me curiously for a moment. "They are two different worlds."

I look at him as I try to figure this out. I'm not sure what he means by worlds...maybe different dimensions? "So this world and the human world are two different places. When you say the reef is a border...what do you mean?"

"The reef is where the two worlds touch."

My eyes go wide. He must mean like another dimension. "So, you can go into the human world?"

He nods as he eats an oyster. "Yes, I can go into the human world just as you came into my world."

I nibble on a crab, lost in thought. This is so much information. Worlds and dimensions and different types of Guardians—it's overwhelming. My heart starts racing and my chest feels tight, like I can't breathe.

I force myself to take a deep breath to calm the anxiety I can feel growing inside me. I remind myself that I just need to focus on the problem at hand—all that bigger stuff doesn't matter. It doesn't matter if I'm in a different dimension or on a different planet. I'm in a place that isn't the human world.

I finally say, "So, the problem is that my disappearance brought too many humans. Then one of them saw you and now more have shown up. Too many for you to fight?"

He nods.

The local search and rescue team looking for me probably reported seeing an octopus man to authorities. I'm willing to bet that the new people that are bringing out equipment and are interested in the reef are government agents. Shit...that's probably not good.

"So, if there are too many, can't you get one of those magic water Guardians to come fight them?"

He shakes his head. "They are not that common. The one that performs all of our ceremonies is the only one that I know of for a great distance. We have a way to call for aid. It will bring all of the Guardians nearby to help defend against a human invasion. It will also call him, but I have no way of knowing where he is and how long it will take to get him here."

"But you can call for help, right? Ovaggd'tho and others will come to help? Would Xaiolpa fight?" Somehow, I can't imagine Xaiolpa fighting. She's muscular and obviously strong, but she's so bubbly and sunny.

He nods while chewing another crab. "Yes, they'll come. Of course Xaiolpa would fight. Our females are strong and fierce." He pauses for a minute, thinking. "I think I'll likely have to call for aid tomorrow. The way the humans are acting is concerning me. They aren't usually this interested in the reef."

I sigh. "They're probably special humans. Dealing with your kind is probably what they do."

He furrows his brow. "What do you mean?"

"You said that some of your people have been taken by humans. Well, the humans that took them would be specially trained humans. Likely ones that are working for a government." I glance at him realizing that he may not know what a government is, and he looks confused. "Um...working for the people that rule our land. They probably know about you already and are wanting to capture another one of you."

He nods. "That's what I fear too."

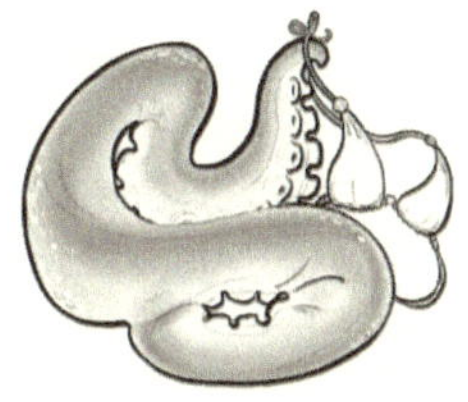

Chapter 20

Naomi

We sit quietly for a few minutes, both lost in thought.

Octo finally pulls a handful of something out of his net. "Here, Naomi, try one of these."

He opens his hand and has a couple of sea urchins in it. He cracks one open and hands it to me. I take it carefully. Then he cracks the other open. I watch as he scoops the yellow contents out with his fingers and eats it, so I do the same.

I practically moan as I eat it. "Oh, my gods, this is delicious, Octo! Thank you for bringing me one."

He pulls another one out of the bag and cracks it open, then hands it to me. "Here, you eat this one too."

I take it greedily from his hands and scoop it into my mouth. It's so good. It's creamy and a little bit sweet.

Octo eyes me with appreciation.

With dinner done, Octo folds his net back up and puts it in its pouch. Then he cleans up the leftover shells and throws them out of the ship.

He looks at me and asks, "Do you need to use your *bathroom* before we sleep?"

I shake my head. "I used it while Xaiolpa was here."

I don't tell him that she probably thinks I'm crazy now. She was so bewildered and concerned by me needing to go into the other room and hide in order to relieve myself. She tried to follow me in.

He settles down in the nest, then I swim over to him, lay my body on top of his, and wrap my arms around him. He wraps his arms and tentacles around me.

"Thank you for not locking me in the cage today. I had a nice day with Xaiolpa."

He nuzzles his mouth into the gills on the side of my neck, and he kisses them lightly. They're so sensitive, it sends a bolt of longing through me. I turn my head and kiss him.

I feel his hand graze up my side to cup my breast. He pinches my nipple between his thumb and forefinger, and I whimper.

Huskily he says, "This morning you used your mouth on me. Does that mean that it's acceptable for me to use my mouth on you?"

I let out another little whimper at the thought of that, then I nod.

He grabs me by the hips and begins to slide me up his torso and over his shoulders until I'm hovering over his mouth. I feel some of his tentacles sliding up my legs. As he wraps his strong arms around my thighs to hold me to him, I feel his tongue slide through the folds of my pussy.

"Oh fuck, Octo!"

He growls, then begins to lick me with abandon. It's like he's been unleashed on me and can't get enough. I moan and buck against him, but he holds me tightly in place. The tentacles sliding up my legs slide straight for my pussy. I feel each of them slip into me as Octo focuses on licking my clit. I'm so lost in my pleasure that I can barely think.

They begin thrusting into me hard and fast. I'm nearly screaming it feels so good. I feel another tentacle snake up my leg and then it prods against my butt gently. I keen as it carefully presses into me. He's slow and gentle with it, and it feels amazing.

I whimper and moan and gasp as he works me with his tongue and tentacles. Finally, he growls against my clit, and my orgasm explodes through me. I writhe and spasm wave after wave of pleasure rolls through me.

Once the aftershocks of my orgasm have subsided, and my muscles feel limp, the tentacles inside me slowly slip out. Octo uses more of his tentacles to gently lower me from his mouth and slide me right onto his cock.

I whine as his cock sinks into me. "Oh, fuck, Octo."

He cups my face with his hands and kisses me as he pulls his hips back and snaps them back to thrust into me. His tentacles hold me in place as he fucks me.

My breath hitches as his kisses leave my mouth and begin trailing onto my gills. Little sparks of pleasure shoot through me. They combine with the pleasure in my belly from each of his thrusts.

I moan his name, and he begins kissing my chest and I arch my back as his mouth latches onto my breast. I can feel him teasing my nipple with his tongue while he steadily fucks me.

I cry out with each thrust. Then I feel one of his tentacles snake around my hips and down towards my pussy. One of the suckers latches onto my clit and I cry out. "Fuck, Octo!"

He continues to pound into me while working his mouth on my nipple and his sucker on my clit. An orgasm rips through me, and I cry out as my body thrashes and spasms against him. My pussy pulses around his cock, milking him, and then he's yelling as he comes and fills me with his seed.

We're both breathless by the time we come down from our orgasms. Octo kisses me deeply, when he pulls back from my mouth, he strokes my cheek with his claw. "Naomi, you are my perfect mate."

I kiss him back and whisper, "Thank you," onto his lips.

He pulls me down onto his torso. "Come, let's sleep."

Chapter 21

My Naomi sleeps pressed against my chest with my arms around her. She's still asleep when I wake early in the morning. Sometime during the night, she rolled over so that her back is against my chest.

I don't wake her. I just lay there, holding her while she slumbers. I gently stroke my claws over her, and my hand hovers over her stomach. I press it flat against her belly. I don't know if I'm able to put young in her. Truthfully, I have not thought much about it.

I know that Ovaggd'tho and Xaiolpa have opted to wait to have young so they could enjoy some time together first. My people tend to have a lot of young very quickly, so they went to a healer to delay it. But I don't know about Naomi and I. Would we have a lot of young like my people? I don't even know how many humans have. And she's not even human anymore. We ought to go to a healer and see what they say.

Naomi stretches and groans. When she opens her eyes, she rolls over and looks at me and smiles, "Hi."

I say, "Did you sleep well?"

She yawns. "Mhmm."

"Good. We should get up, Ovaggd'tho and Xaiolpa should be here soon."

She gives me a concerned look. "He's going with you to see what's happening at the beach?"

I nod.

She's quiet for a few minutes. "Can Xaiolpa and I come too?"

I sigh. I can't let her come, and I know she's going to be mad about it.

Before I can refuse her, she quickly says, "Wait, just hear me out. Please."

I nod.

"I actually know things about humans and how they work. I've never been a part of a search and rescue team, but I can watch them and tell you what I think they're doing and if you need to be worried. And Xaiolpa can stay with me. Didn't you say she was a fighter? She can help keep me safe. If something happens, she can get me out of there and bring me back here."

I have to admit, it's not a terrible plan. I don't like the idea of Naomi being there, but if I have to call for help like I think I will, then Xaiolpa will just have to bring her anyway.

"Hmmm. It does sound like a good plan."

Naomi gives me a huge smile. "Really? You'll let me come with you?"

I nod. "Yes, I would like your opinion on what the humans are doing."

She hugs then kisses me. I wrap my arms around her and deepen the kiss.

When she pulls away, she says, "Thank you, Octo, for letting me help."

Just then, I hear Ovaggd'tho and Xaiolpa talking as they swim up to the ship. When they get to the broken windows, Xaiolpa says, "Good Morning!" while Ovaggd'tho nods to us. He's holding both his and Xaiolpa's spears and has a serious look on his face. He's prepared to do whatever we have to.

Naomi smiles at her. "Guess what—we're going with them today!"

Ovaggd'tho and Xaiolpa both give me a surprised look.

In confirmation, I say, "She can offer us insight into what the humans are doing."

Xaiolpa smiles. "This is going to be so exciting! Are you nervous, Naomi? Don't worry, if they have to fight, I'll keep you safe."

I look at Xaiolpa. "If we have to fight, then get her back here."

She nods. "Of course."

I get up and grab my spear, then look at Naomi. "Are you ready?"

She gives me a wide-eyed look, but nods. I take her hand, and we swim out of our home.

Ovaggd'tho gives Xaiolpa her spear, and we all swim in the direction of the beach.

As we're swimming, Naomi says, "Do I get a spear some day?"

I shake my head, "No."

She sighs in exasperation. "But—"

"No, Naomi. You have to know how to use a spear to be able to have one."

"How do you know that I can't use a spear?"

I know what she's doing, so I say, "Do you?"

"No, but you can't just tell me no without asking me that first."

I sigh.

She's quiet for a bit, then she says, "What if you taught me how to use one?"

I think about it for a minute. "Maybe. But I don't like the idea of my mate fighting."

She smirks at me. "I was good at fighting you. Maybe I'm a good fighter."

I just snort.

We swim in silence. My mind is too focused on what we may be swimming into to talk more.

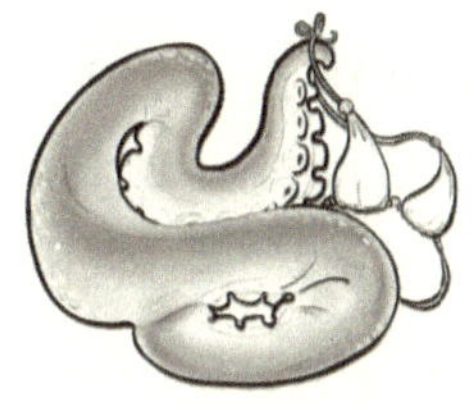

Chapter 22

Naomi

Octo is quiet as we swim toward the beach. He holds on strongly to my hand, though. I imagine he's focused on the human situation and is worried about what we will encounter when we get there. I stay quiet so I don't disturb him.

Ovaggd'tho and Xaiolpa are similarly quiet.

I look at everything we pass as we swim by. Nothing really stands out as different than what I saw when we visited Ovaggd'tho and Xaiolpa's home.

I see another kelp forest and lots of little sea creatures and fish. There are several small coral reefs. As we swim, we pass over a large black manta ray as it gracefully glides through the water. We also pass several large, green sea turtles as they slowly swim through a swarm of translucent pink jellyfish, eating as many as they can.

After we have been swimming for a short while, I realize that Octo is slowing down and I look in front of us and gasp as I discover a massive, beautiful coral reef. It's covered in patches of bright colors and interesting shapes. Brightly colored fish swim all over it, darting between and under pieces of coral.

"Oh my gods, is this the reef at the border?"

Octo nods.

"It's beautiful!"

We are only a few feet away from it, but I look at Octo and say, "Can I get closer?"

"Yes."

I swim right up to the coral and accidentally startle a group of bright yellow fish near a large pale red anemone. The anemone is home to a pair of beautiful black and white clown fish that are swimming through its tentacles. Nearby, there are several large, flat, red fans that look like they are made of lace, and behind those are the reaching branches of pale-yellow coral. There are clumps of blue and green corals that look like little starbursts, and more of the squiggly yellow ones that look like brains. There are spikey clumps of corals in blues and pinks and purples, and fans of creams and greens and oranges. Intermixed among all the corals are clumps of the long tubes that the featherlike tails of worms poke out of, gently swaying in the water filtering out their microscopic meals.

Behind a fan of coral, I notice two tiny crabs caught in a tug-o-war battle over a small scrap of food. Each crab is pinched onto the piece and refuses to let go. Another movement catches my eye, and I see the head of a terrifying-looking eel with sharp teeth sticking out from a small burrow surrounded by spikes of colorful coral waiting for a meal to swim by.

I'm still looking at everything when Octo says, "Naomi, come. I'll show you where we can best see the beach."

I follow him. He takes us over to an area that has a large formation of coral that we can hide behind and peek over the top of. He looks over first and shakes his head at what he sees.

Ovaggd'tho and Xaiolpa look over next. When they duck back down, they have grim looks on their faces. I gather my courage and look over the top of the coral next. I hold my hair down so that it doesn't float around my head and give away our hiding spot.

What I see is bad. There are a lot of boats and divers. Octo is right—they seem very interested in the reef. In fact, I would say that's the only thing they're interested in. They don't look like they're searching for a person or a body. They're here for the reef. Even more concerning is the equipment they have brought down. They have things that are clearly measuring something in the reef. I see dials, cords, and digital displays. It reminds me of those ghost chaser shows where they bring stuff in to read energy and supernatural stuff. All of the drivers are wearing black wet-suits and I'm pretty sure they have weapons strapped to them.

While taking all of this in, I whisper, "Shit. Shit-shit-shit."

I duck back down behind the coral.

Octo takes one look at my face. "This is bad, isn't it?"

"Yes. I don't think they're looking for me or my body. They're specifically interested in the reef. They've also brought down equipment to measure something...like magic, maybe. I don't know if they can measure magic, but I think they know this reef is some sort of barrier or has some type of magical or supernatural power."

I peek over the coral again to get my bearings on where we are.

I look back and ask Octo, "Is this the beach you took me from?"

"Yes."

I look toward the beach again. It's weird seeing it from this angle and underwater, but I'm starting to get my bearings. I try to remember the direction I came from when I walked down to the alcove. I look to my left and see a rocky area. That must be the underwater portion of the wall I had to go through to get to the alcove.

I duck back behind the coral again.

"Can we go that way?" I point in the direction I would've come from when I walked on the beach from the hotel.

Octo nods. "You think something over there is important?"

"I don't know. I just feel like we should go over there, like we're supposed to. If they were really looking for me, they would be over there too."

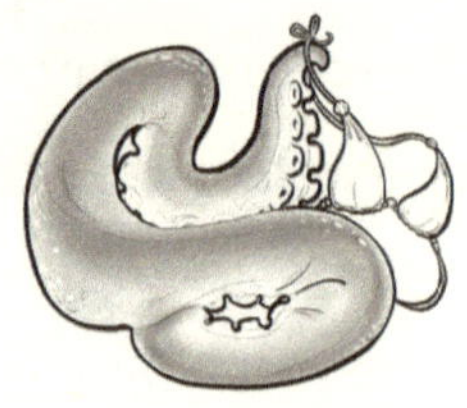

Chapter 23

Naomi

We swim down the reef in the direction of the hotel. Octo occasionally pops his head out of the water to check where we are, and once we are in the right place, he tells us to stop swimming.

I carefully peek over the reef and don't see any swimmers. Actually, I don't see anyone in the water. I look at Octo, "I'm going to poke my head above water to see what's happening on the beach."

He startles when I say that and then shakes his head violently. "No, Naomi, it's too dangerous! I will look and tell you what I see."

I shake my head. "I'll be careful, Octo. You need my input on this, so you need me to see it with my own eyes.

I promise I'll be careful. Plus, you're here to protect me if anything happens."

He watches me for a minute, but I can tell that he knows I'm right. Finally, he just nods.

I swim up to the surface with Octo right behind me. Once I get to the surface, I slowly push my head out of the water. The first thing I notice is the breeze on my face. It feels so cold and alien, and it's then that I realize I haven't had my head above water in *days*. For some reason it feels wrong now. The air burns my nostrils, but I seem to still be able to breathe through my nose. It isn't comfortable, though. My gills also feel very exposed and sensitive when they're out of the water.

I try to ignore the strange sensations and look at the shore, but I don't see anyone. If agents are looking for me, it seems like there should be some over here. This is the hotel I was staying at. I'm looking around when movement up by the hotel catches my eye, and I look there.

It's Cindy and her fiancé, Nathan. They're on the patio surrounding the hotel. Nathan is leaning on his elbows on the railing, looking in the direction of the agents. He's always been effortlessly attractive in that tall, dark, and handsome sort of way. Right now, he just looks exhausted. Cindy is standing beside him. Her arms are crossed over her chest and she's bouncing her leg a little. Her long brown hair is pulled into a ponytail, and her skin looks perfectly sun-kissed. She's wearing a white bikini with a sheer coverup over it. I can tell from the way she's holding her shoulders and bouncing her leg that she's pissed. She's really pissed. She's also looking toward where the agents are supposedly looking for me.

Suddenly she starts flinging her arms toward the alcove and saying something to Nathan. She must be angry about how they're handling my disappearance. I'm sure she's giving him an earful about it.

I watch her, completely mesmerized. Cindy has been my best friend forever. We've gone to the same school since kindergarten. We even went to the same college. We were roommates through college, and continued to share an apartment after graduation. We made sure to both find jobs near each other so we could continue to live together. Once we were both more established with our careers and making a bit more money, we upgraded to a nicer apartment but still remained roommates. Shortly after my thirtieth birthday, she met Nathan and after a whirlwind romance, they moved in together. Now, it's a year later and they're getting married.

My heart aches just from looking at her. She's more like a sister to me than a friend at this point. I miss her so much that it physically hurts. I can feel tears stinging behind my eyes, and I blink them back. There will be time for that later.

Cindy is still flailing her arms and complaining about the agents. I shake my head and smile at that thought. I'm sure she has given them hell. Cindy is a force to be reckoned with.

I've had my head above water for a few minutes now, and I don't want to risk getting caught, so I take one last look at Cindy before I go back underwater. Suddenly Cindy turns and looks directly at me. Our eyes lock, and I know she's seen me. She gives me a look of shock. Then she screams, "Naomi!!"

She immediately starts running to the walkway to come down from the hotel to the beach.

I quickly duck my head underwater and say, "Oh shit!"

Octo is right there beside me. "What is it Naomi, did something happen?"

I nod, with tears stinging my eyes. "My best friend, Cindy, she was up there. She saw me. She's running toward the beach."

Octo pushes his head up out of the water and sees Cindy and Nathan running toward the water. He says, "We must go."

Ovaggd'tho and Xaiolpa give us a worried look and we all turn to swim back toward the alcove. Just then, Octo lets out a guttural growl unlike anything I've ever heard from him before. All of his muscles go taut, and he growls, "They've crossed the reef."

Octo grabs the stone on his necklace and says some words in a language that I don't understand. I feel some sort of energy wave come from his necklace, and then it begins glowing. The glow pulses slowly.

I look over at Xaiolpa and Ovaggd'tho and see that their necklaces have also started pulsing and glowing in response to his.

Octo looks at Xaiolpa. "Take Naomi home and keep her safe."

Xaiolpa nods. I grab onto Octo's arm. "No, please. Octo...I can't leave you."

He gently grabs my jaw in his clawed hand and tilts my head up toward him. He kisses me, then says, "Naomi, you must. It's safer for me if I know you're safe. I won't fight as well if I'm worried about you."

I nod and kiss him one more time, then he and Ovaggd'tho swim toward the alcove.

We watch them swim off, then finally Xaiolpa quietly says, "Come, Naomi, we must go."

I look at her and see how miserable and afraid she is. She's just as afraid for Ovaggd'tho as I am for Octo. I look toward the direction they swam away in.

"I don't know about you, but I can't sit around wondering if they are okay. We have to follow them." Then I start swimming after them.

Xaiolpa comes after me. "Naomi, we must go. I promised. You heard what Octhogh'xu said. In order for them to fight well, we must go."

Despite her words, we're both still swimming after them.

Once we are close enough, I can see several humans swimming over the reef in the distance. Octo and Ovaggd'tho are crouched hidden in a pocket of the reef.

Several other Guardians begin to arrive. Octo mentioned that there are many types of Guardians, but all of these look like him and Ovaggd'tho.

Octo turns and sees us, so I swim as fast as I can toward him. I fling myself into his arms and nearly sob. "Octo, I'm afraid."

He hugs me tightly, then in the most gravelly voice I've ever heard come from him, he says, "Naomi, you must go. This was the deal."

I nod, fighting back tears. I'm so afraid for him. I can't lose him. Without him, I would be alone down here—but it's more than that. I want to be with him. I want his company and companionship. I want what we have made over the last few days. He takes care of me and sees me in a way that no one ever has. I care about him and I like him.

Suddenly I realize...am I falling in love with him?

Xaiolpa swims up beside me and interrupts these thoughts. I watch her give Ovaggd'tho a meaningful look. She reaches out and grasps his hand. "Fight well, my love."

Then Xaiolpa grabs my forearm and pulls me away from Octo. "Come, Naomi, we must go to protect them."

I'm sniffling as I let her pull me away. She pulls me for a minute or two, then I begin swimming on my own beside her.

Once we are a good distance away from the reef, I stop and look back. I can still make out Octo and Ovaggd'tho. The other Guardians are grouped around him, and he's updating everyone on the situation. My heart swells with pride for him. He looks strong and in control.

Xaiolpa gently grabs my arm and says, "Come, we must go."

I turn to her. "Can we watch from here? We're far enough away. I can't bear the idea of sitting at home just wondering what's happening."

She sighs and looks back toward the reef. She glances around at where we are, and then she nods. There's a kelp forest near us, she gestures toward it. "We hide in there if any humans begin coming our way."

I nod. "Thank you, Xaiolpa."

She's quiet for a minute, then she says, "I don't want to leave my Ovaggd'tho either."

It looks like they have six other Guardians there to help them, so there are eight of them in total. I don't know how many are needed for a fight, and I hope that's enough.

I see the moment that the humans spot the Guardians and turn toward them. One of them points at the Guardians and they begin swimming toward Octo and his group. I see something shoot from one of the divers toward one of the Guardians. The Guardian easily dodges it. It takes me a moment to realize that the divers must have spear guns. I gasp and cover my mouth in horror. They're shooting at Octo with spears?!

Xaiolpa rubs her hand on my shoulder. "It will be okay, Naomi; they know how to handle this."

The other diver shoots at them too, and it grazes past Octo. There's an explosion of movement as Octo and Ovaggd'tho launch themselves toward the divers.

Octo immediately impales the first one on his spear. He pulls it free as the diver begins sinking into the deep, leaving a trail of blood to mix in with the water.

Ovaggd'tho stabs the second one.

Oh gods. I didn't think about them needing to kill humans. But, I don't see any other way for them to protect this world. You certainly can't tell humans just to go home and forget about this place. Unless they're killed, they'll be back.

Octo and Ovaggd'tho both swim over the reef and into the human territory. The other Guardians follow them.

There's a flurry of motion from the other side of the reef. I catch myself swimming a little bit closer so that I can see. Xaiolpa comes up beside me. I look at her to see if I'm about to get in trouble, but her eyes are riveted on Ovaggd'tho.

I see Octo stab a couple of divers. Two of the Guardians are trying to take down one of the boats idling near the reef. They're underneath it wrapping tentacles around it. It's surreal; it looks like a small-scale version of those drawings of a kraken wrapping up on a ship.

I notice something shooting into the water and I swim straight up to the surface to poke my head out and see what the humans on the boats are doing. When I get my head above water, I see that the people on the boats also have spear guns, and they're shooting them into the water to try to hit the Guardians.

I dive back down to Xaiolpa, and she gasps as a spear grazes Ovaggd'tho's shoulder. I see a tiny line of dark blood as it whisps out of him and into the water.

Near Ovaggd'tho, I see the body of another Guardian suddenly jerk back like someone hit him. He turns in the water, and I see a small spear sticking out of his shoulder. I gasp as he bares his teeth, rage and hatred on his face, then with a mighty thrust of his tentacles, he launches himself at the nearest boat.

The rest of the Guardians realize that there are humans attacking them from above, so they change tactics and begin attacking the boats. In pairs, they get underneath the boats and try to capsize them.

One pair of Guardians has already been successful. The humans fall into the water as the boat flips over. The Guardians grab them and drag them down as they stab them.

Just as another boat is about to flip, I see a spear stab through one of the Guardian's tentacles. I see him yell, then he attacks the boat in a frenzy. The boat flips over and all of the humans fall into the water.

The water is full of splashing with red blooming every-where. Even through all of that, I'm able to keep an eye on where Octo is.

He swims over to one of the boats and pulls himself partially out of the water and onto the boat in an attempt to either flip it or attack the humans.

Then I see his whole body jolt as if stunned and he begins limply sliding back into the water. The humans thrust their arms underwater, grab him, and begin dragging him into the boat.

I scream.

Forgetting about Xaiolpa and everything else, I immediately start swimming for the reef. Most of Octo's body is already out of the water. Just his tentacles are still underwater, and they look strangely limp. I'm screaming on the inside. Oh gods, what did they do to him?

I go to the surface and see the men dragging Octo into the boat. Once they have his shoulders and chest over the side of the boat, he flops the rest of the way in and is still.

I watch all of this in slow motion horror. No—he can't be dead. He can't. I would know, wouldn't I? I search within my chest, feeling for that pull between us. I panic for a moment because I can't find it. But then the men start their boat and steer it toward the other side of the alcove, taking Octo even further from me, and I feel it. I feel the pull of the magic that's bound us together. He's alive! He has to be.

I swim to the reef, and once I reach it, I swim as hard and as fast as I can along it, following the path of the boat as best I can while staying behind the safety of the reef. I pass the alcove area and I discover that another, much larger beach stretches out before me. There are a few vehicles on this beach. There's a big white truck like a moving truck, and a few pickup trucks with boat trailers on them. This must be where they launched their boats from.

As the boat pulls up into the shallow water, agents begin opening up the back of the large truck. Several of them unload something from the truck that looks like a cross between a stretcher and a hammock.

Six agents begin to carry it to the water.

I gasp, "Shit!" They're going to transport him. That sling thing is how they're going to carry him. If they get him out of the water and into that van, I'll never see him again. I feel the sting of tears in my eyes. I can feel my heart racing and my chest feels tight.

Out loud, but still to myself, I say, "No—this isn't the time to panic." I take a deep breath, then suddenly I know what I need to do.

I dart off back toward the alcove, swimming as fast as I can. I pass it and see that Guardians are still fighting humans. I swim straight to the stretch of beach by the hotel. I poke my head above water and see that Cindy and Nathan are still standing on the beach. Cindy has waded knee-deep into the water, and I can see her searching the horizon for a glimpse of me.

I swim over the reef and straight to Cindy. As soon as I'm close to her, I pop my head out of the water and gasping for air, I rasp, "Cindy!"

Cindy screams and stumbles backwards, falling into the water. She scrambles back up and slowly steps backwards away from me.

She stares at me wide-eyed, then she finally says, "Naomi?"

I nod. I press my body down into the water so my neck is underwater, and my gills can breathe. I swam so hard that I'm out of breath and I'm gasping. I take a few large breaths through my gills, then I say, "It's me, Cindy, it's me."

Tears fill her eyes and begin running down her face. "Naomi...what happened? What is this? I don't understand. Are you some sort of mermaid?" She pauses for a second. "Are you naked?"

"I met my mate. My *mate*, Cindy." With my hand, I gesture toward my body. "This is because of him, so I can live with him in the water. I'll explain it all later, I promise. But I need help. The agents have captured him." A sob escapes me. "They have captured my mate, Cindy. Please help me. I love him."

The moment the words come out of my mouth, I realize they're true. I love him. I haven't even known him that long—and he kidnapped me. I don't know, maybe the mating bond is pushing it along. But I love him. He's my mate.

Cindy stares at me with wide eyes.

She continues to stand there staring at me as I say, "Please, Cindy, help me."

That snaps her out of it. She nods once. "Where are they?"

I point in the direction I came from. "They're on another beach just beyond the alcove. They're going to load him up in a truck and take him." I choke back a sob.

She nods and quickly walks out of the water then breaks into a run in the sand. "Come on Nathan, we have to help Naomi!"

I realize then that Nathan has just been staring at me slack-jawed this whole time. He shakes his head and runs after Cindy. I faintly hear him say, "Was she naked?"

I swim back away from the beach, over the reef, and nearly swim into Xaiolpa.

"Naomi! What happened? Where's Octo?"

I let out a sob. "They have him. They're going to take him! I'm getting my friend to help."

Xaiolpa gasps, "A human?!"

But I don't wait for her to say anything else. I begin swimming along the reef, frequently popping my head above water, following Cindy's progress.

Cindy runs into the alcove. Two agents immediately run up to intercept her, but no one is going to stop Cindy when she's on a mission. She dodges them and continues running.

The Guardians are still fighting in the water, and an agent begins screaming for help. This stops the agents that are chasing Cindy. They must realize that the Guardians are a much larger threat than one little woman. So, they quit pursuing Cindy and run toward the water, trying to get to the screaming agent.

Cindy makes it through the alcove and runs out onto the other beach.

The agents are carrying Octo in the sling, trying to get him loaded into the truck. He must be heavy because it's taking four men to carry him, and a couple more have climbed into the truck trying to pull him up into some sort of low walled container.

Cindy immediately starts yelling at the agents. She's screaming and pointing towards Octo, but I can't hear anything that she's saying.

A couple of agents intercept her and keep her away from the truck. I can tell they're trying to calm her down, but she's still acting frantic and yelling at them.

I decide to risk swimming over the reef to be closer to the beach so I can hear what's being said. I stay close against the rocky wall dividing off the alcove as I slink forward in the water until I can hear.

Once I'm finally close enough to hear them talking, I hear Cindy yell, "Is that what happened to my friend? Did that thing take her?"

I can only hear a murmuring response from the agent. I creep closer until I can hear the agent more clearly.

Cindy is being loud and demanding, trying to bully this guy into letting her get near Octo. "I want to talk to it!!"

The agent calmly says, "Ma'am, you can't talk to it. It's a dangerous creature. It's also asleep so we can get it to our facility."

Cindy scoffs. "Well, then I'll come to the facility. I want to talk to that fucking thing and find out where my friend is!"

"I understand, ma'am, we are working to find out where she is."

"Bullshit! I don't believe you. I bet all you want is that octopus guy so you can run experiments on him. You aren't going to try to find Naomi. This whole operation obviously isn't about Naomi! I want to talk to that thing and ask it where she is!" Cindy yells.

She's in full on 'Karen' mode now. I'm surprised she hasn't demanded this guy's superior yet.

The agent sighs, "Let me see what I can do. Stay right here while I go ask my boss."

The agent walks toward the truck and has a conversation with another agent that's overseeing getting Octo into the truck. They exchange a few words, and both look over toward Cindy. The supervisor sighs heavily and shakes his head, then he walks a few steps away to make a phone call. After a brief conversation, he walks back to the agent. They both turn their backs to Cindy and, unknowingly, to me. Whatever they're saying, they don't want her to see their expressions or read their lips. After a quick exchange, the agent nods at this superior and then turns back facing Cindy's direction.

He walks back over to Cindy. "Ma'am, you can come to the facility and try to talk to it."

Cindy loudly exclaims, "Finally! Where's the facility?"

The agent points up the beach and past the hotel. He tells Cindy to take the road left out of the hotel parking lot. Then drive until she sees it. There will be big gates, she won't be able to miss it. "When you get to the gates, just buzz on the intercom and we'll let you in."

"Thank you." She makes a show of throwing her hands in the air and says, "Finally someone helpful."

Just as Cindy turns and walks back toward the alcove, I hear a garbled yell from Octo. I look over at the truck and see him start to thrash in his sling. Before I can even react, someone jabs a syringe into him and injects him with something. He immediately goes limp again.

I cover my mouth so I won't scream or sob. I remind myself that I can't do anything here. I have to keep myself safe right now.

I quickly swim back toward the reef and meet Xaiolpa and Ovaggd'tho there.

Xaiolpa says, "Did you find out where they're taking him?"

"Yes." I look at Ovaggd'tho. He has a few bloody gashes, but he looks okay. "Are they still fighting?"

Ovaggd'tho shakes his head. "No, we were able to kill some and drive the rest back to the beach. I worry they will come back with reinforcements though." Just then, a handful of agents come running out of the alcove. One of them is helping a limping diver. Another is calling for a first aid kit.

We don't need to stay here. "Come on. Let's meet up with my friend by the hotel." Then we swim along the reef toward it.

As soon as we pass the wall into the calm waters of the alcove, the water becomes thick and dark with blood. I can taste the metallic tang of it in my gills. I stop and look around in horror. I can see all of the bodies floating near the beach. I make a strangled gasping sound, and feel the bile rise up in the back of my throat. This really was a battle.

I'm frozen in horror and can't stop staring, but suddenly I feel something brush past me. I look down and see a shark swimming toward the beach. I look around and see other dark shapes swimming this way.

Ovaggd'tho grabs my attention. "Come, we should get away from here. The sharks will have a frenzy soon."

I keep glancing around horrified. But all those people... I take a deep breath and try to remind myself that these are the bad guys. They're trying to kidnap Octo. It's them or us.

I nod and follow Xaiolpa and Ovaggd'tho.

The water clears up as we pass the wall. I stick my head above water to find Cindy. She's waiting for me in the same spot I found her earlier.

I duck back down and say, "I'm going to swim up to the beach and talk to my friend. We need to make a plan to get Octo." Xaiolpa and Ovaggd'tho both nod.

I quickly swim up to Cindy. She gasps when I pop my head above water this time.

Cindy jumps. "Oh gods, Naomi, I was so scared you were a shark or something."

This reminds me of the day Octo told me that humans were more afraid of sharks than we needed to be. I can feel the tears threatening to fall, and it takes me a minute to blink them back.

Cindy watches me curiously, then she says, "Don't worry, Naomi, we'll get him back."

I sniff a little and nod.

"Did you hear what the agent said?"

I nod again.

"Nathan and I will run up to our room and change, then we'll drive over there. I think I know what building he's talking about. I think it backs up to the water, so you should be able to follow along in the water."

I take a deep breath and ask, "Do you have a plan?"

She shakes her head. "No, I don't. I'm just going to have to wing it once we get inside."

I must give her a worried look because she smiles and says, "Oh, Naomi, we'll get your tentacled man back, I promise. Has anyone ever been able to stop me from doing something that I wanted to do?"

I smile at that. She always manages to get her way.

"Give Nathan and I a few minutes, and then we'll be on our way."

I nod. "I have some friends with me too. We'll start making our way to the facility. Cindy...thank you. I know this is a lot to take in."

Tears begin running down Cindy's cheeks. "Oh, Naomi, I don't care what you look like; I'm just glad to have my best friend back."

She leans down to give me a hug, and I hug her back.

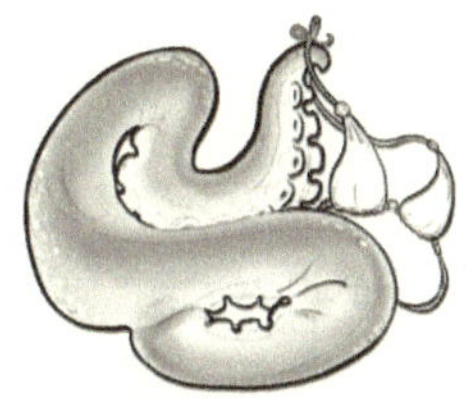

Chapter 24

Naomi

Once Cindy stands and walks back to Nathan on the beach, I turn and swim toward the reef and Xaiolpa and Ovaggd'tho.

When I reach them, Xaiolpa says, "Was that your friend?"

I nod, and sniff a little. "Yes. She's been my best friend for most of my life. We met when we were young children and we've been practically inseparable until now. She's getting married to the man that was standing on the beach. That's why I'm here. It was supposed to be a beach wedding." I smile and shake my head. "Octo kind of made a mess of that plan."

Xaiolpa asks, "What's a wedding?"

I'm startled by the question, but it makes sense when I think about it. Octo's people don't have weddings; they just do the mating bite thing.

"It's a ceremony for taking someone as your mate. You say vows to each other in front of everyone. It's a human custom."

Xaiolpa exclaims, "Oh I like that! A ceremony and making vows to your mate. That sounds lovely, Naomi."

I give her a small smile and say, "It is."

Xaiolpa then gives me a knowing grin and says, "I also like how you call Octhogh'xu 'Octo'."

I give her a startled look. I didn't even think about the fact that I wasn't using his full name. I groan, "He hates me calling him that, he's going to be so embarrassed when he finds out I've been calling him that in front of his friends."

Xaiolpa smiles. "Well, I think it's sweet. Maybe I'll come up with a sweet name for my mate as well." She glances at Ovaggd'tho.

He shakes his head and smiles back at her. "I would be honored to have any name that you chose to call me."

We all smile for a moment, then the moment sobers.

Looking at them, I say, "We have to save him. I don't know what I'll do if..." I can't finish the thought.

Ovaggd'tho gives me a pitying look. Xaiolpa says, "Don't worry, Naomi, Octhogh'xu is a strong warrior. One of the strongest. We'll get him back."

I nod then say, "We should get on our way. My friend, Cindy, said they're taking him to a facility just up the beach. Cindy and her fiancé are going there to try to get Octo out. It's supposed to back up to the water, so hopefully we can see what's going on and maybe help."

I begin to swim in the direction of the facility. Xaiolpa and Ovaggd'tho follow me.

After a few minutes, Xaiolpa catches up to me and says, "We'll be swimming through other Guardians' territories to get there. Ovaggd'tho is going to recruit those Guardians to help us. I'll keep swimming with you, and they'll meet us there.

I nod. "Thank you Xaiolpa, I don't know what I would do without you and Ovaggd'tho."

She just smiles and says, "That's what friends are for."

We swim for probably about ten minutes. The reef runs along this beach too, and we have been careful to stay on the Guardian side, but I begin to notice a strange shape underwater on the human side.

It's just a shadow at first, but it kind of looks like a building that's been built underwater. As we get closer, I realize that's exactly what it is. There's a building that has a lower level below the water level. This must be the facility.

I stop swimming as we near it and rise up to the surface. When I pop my head out of the water, I'm confronted with a massive building. There's a large patio in the back that overlooks the water. Below the water, there are giant windows as if there is a viewing room down there.

I look towards the building's parking lot, but I don't see Cindy and Nathan's car yet. I go back below the surface and tell Xaiolpa that they haven't arrived yet.

"I'll wait with my head above water to watch for Cindy. You wait down here for Ovaggd'tho and whatever Guardians he's able to recruit."

Ovaggd'tho and the Guardians end up arriving before Cindy and Nathan. Xaiolpa taps on my leg when they're here, and I duck back into the water to meet them.

There are five male Guardians that all look like Octo and Ovaggd'tho. Xaiolpa introduces me to all of them. I'm so stressed out about Octo that I can't remember any of their names.

As soon as I can, I pop my head back above water. I'm just in time to see Cindy getting out of her car. I see her scan the surface until she sees me. She doesn't make any sort of visible sign that she's seen me, but I know she has.

I watch as they walk up to the building.

Once she disappears from sight, I slip back underwater and tell the others that my friend is here. Xaiolpa leads me over to a male that looks like his entire body is made of blue crystal, and his eyes are pupilless and glow blue. He has long flowing hair that's the same blue as his skin. He's beautiful in an alien way. Before introducing me, she subtly whispers in my ear that this is the Sea Guardian that can turn into water.

Louder, she says, "Naomi, this is Vrala."

Then to Vrala she says, "This is Octhogh'xu's new mate, Naomi. She was human when he mated her." He nods to me.

We float there, looking over each other, and I'm completely mesmerized by how crystalline he looks.

A few moments later, I turn back to Xaiolpa and say, "We have to figure out some way to help. There's something underwater at the building. I'm going to swim over there and get a closer look."

She nods. "Be careful, Naomi."

I swim over the reef and up to the building. The patio of the building juts out into the water and has stones built up around it. I dip back underwater and circle to the backside of the patio and see that there's a large window looking into some sort of laboratory.

Inside the lab is a large tank with an open top. Octo swims up to the edge of it and sticks his head above water. He's looking at me with so much sorrow. I press my hand to the glass, and just as I do, a door opens at the back of the room.

Cindy and Nathan walk in and walk down a few steps to the lab floor. I see Cindy gasp and point when she sees me.

An agent walks in behind them, and frowns when he sees me. They exchange a few words; it looks like Cindy is yelling at him. She's pointing toward me in the window. The agent replies back to her and then finally shrugs. I'm able to read his lips when he says, "I don't know." He begins talking to her heatedly and points at Octo's tank. Cindy huffs and throws her hands in the air, then defeated, she nods. The agent leaves the room, leaving Cindy and Nathan alone with Octo.

I notice the agent shut the door on his way out, and I frown because it looks a lot like a submarine door. I wonder if it has one of those wheel latches on the other side. Did he just lock them in?

Chapter 25

Octhogh'xu / Octo

I claw my way back to consciousness and wake up in some sort of glass box full of water. I swim to the sides of it and realize that it's a cage for me.

I can see through the glass walls and I'm in some sort of room made of metal.

I don't see a way out of this situation.

I press my forehead to the glass. Naomi. Poor Naomi, I pulled her into my world just to get captured in hers.

I notice a flicker of movement through the glass and realize that I can see a large window across the room from me that's looking into the water. This room must be underwater.

In that moment, Naomi swims up to the window. I don't know how well she can see into the room, so I stick my head above water to look at her.

She sees me and presses her hand to the glass.

I'm sorry, my Naomi. I'm sorry we only had a short time together.

A door in the room opens and a human female and male walk in along with one of the males that helped capture me. I recognize this female from the searches on the beach.

As soon as she walks into the room, she sees Naomi in the window and gasps and points at her. Then she turns and begins yelling at the agent demanding to know what's going on. She wants to know what happened to her friend, and if that's real.

The male that helped capture me frowns deeply when he sees Naomi in the window, but he doesn't attempt to answer any of the woman's questions. He just shrugs and says he doesn't know what happened. This leads to more yelling from the woman. Finally, the male snaps at her and points to me. "Do you want to talk to him, or not? This is the only chance you'll get."

The woman lets out an irritated huff, then nods.

The male turns to leave and says, "I'll be just outside this door if you need me."

She watches him leave and shut the door, then looks over toward Naomi again. She walks over to the window and presses her hand to the glass. "Don't worry, Naomi, we'll figure out a way to get him out of here."

Is she talking about me? Is she here to rescue me?

She comes back over toward me, then studies me for a moment before she says, "I'm going to help you because I love Naomi, but I know you took her away from me. I know this is your fault, and I need to know why."

I look at her for a moment. I can see the rage in her eyes. For just a moment, I feel like I can't speak while staring down this fearless female. I clear my throat, then say, "I'm sorry. I didn't realize the consequences of my actions. I didn't mean to hurt Naomi or anyone she cares about. I now know that I ripped her from her world and everyone she loved."

The female asks, "But why?"

I sigh and spread my hands out, palms up. "She's my mate. She was meant for me. I scented her when she was walking in the water, and I knew. It's the way my people take a mate. I didn't know that humans didn't do the same."

Her rage cools the smallest bit after I explain it. She stares at me, then says, "You're lucky that she loves you.

You better make her happy. Now, help us figure out a way to get you out of here."

Just then a loud blaring siren goes off and a light begins flashing in the ceiling. Metal panels slide down and cover the human light boxes that are in the walls.

The male runs to the door and tries to open it, but it won't open. He yells, "Hey! Hey! What's going on? We're locked in here!"

No one answers or opens the door.

Suddenly water begins pouring in from openings on either side of the room. I can tell from the scent of the water that it's from the sea.

The female screams and runs over to help her mate bang on the door. She yells at the door. "Let us out! There's water coming in! What are you doing? Let us out! Please!"

Still no answer.

I hear a loud thudding noise and realize it's Naomi, she's beating on the glass, hitting it as hard as she can. She screams, "Cindy!" It sounds muffled from our side.

Cindy runs to the window, "Naomi, they're going to drown us!"

Naomi becomes frantic and hits the glass repeatedly as hard as she can. She eventually yells, "I'm going to get help." Then she swims off.

The male must realize that the humans aren't going to open that door, and he gives up beating on it. He begins searching through the room, frantically looking for something.

The water has risen to nearly their knees as they look around the room.

I climb out of my glass box and drop myself onto the floor.

Cindy's eyes go wide when she sees me and she recoils away from me.

I hold my hands out in a soothing way, "I'm not going to hurt you, I only wish to help."

I use my tentacles to pull myself toward the large window. I hit it with my fist to test it. I can tell it's solid, and it's going to take more than just hitting it to break it.

Ovaggd'tho and Vrala swim up to the window. Ovaggd'tho hits the window with his fist and then tries with his spear. The spear leaves a scratch, but doesn't do more than that.

Vrala then tries to funnel a stream of water at the window. It still does nothing. He starts pushing water harder, and still nothing.

Ovaggd'tho tries hitting it with his spear again. It still only leaves a scratch.

Both Ovaggd'tho and Vrala pause in the assault on the window.

Ovaggd'tho comes up to the glass and yells, "Naomi had an idea. She had to return to where we battled the humans. Xaiolpa went with her to keep her safe."

I see him glance toward the humans, and I look at them. I know what he's trying to communicate. The water level is nearing the tops of their legs. I hope Naomi is able to get back quickly.

Ovaggd'tho then adds, "Other Guardians are climbing the embankment to the building. They're going to attack the humans from the upper level and try to come down to get to you."

I nod at Ovaggd'tho, then I look at the humans. Cindy is crying now and her mate is hugging her. They must have realized that there is no way for us to break out, and we must just wait.

I look at them and say, "Help is coming. We must be patient." Cindy just nods and continues crying.

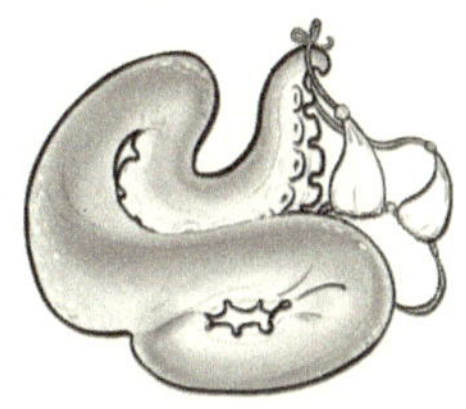

Chapter 26

Naomi

I swim as fast as I can toward the beach where the battle took place. I can hear my pulse pounding in my ears. It feels like it's pounding away the seconds that Cindy and Nathan have left. With that thought, I swim harder. Gods, please let this work.

I'm going back to the beach to find one of those spear guns. That's the only hope we have of breaking that glass.

Xaiolpa follows close behind me. She only came along to make sure that I'm safe. Both she and Ovaggd'tho insisted.

As I swim, I start to taste the metallic tang of all of the blood in the water at the beach. I must be close.

I have to keep going. I can't stop. Cindy needs me. Cindy has always been everything to me. My family was a mess as a kid. Cindy was my rock. She taught me to be strong; she saved me. I never would have survived my childhood without her. I can't lose her now. I *won't* lose her.

And gods, what about Octo? I can't lose him either. But I have to worry about Cindy and Nathan first. Octo will be fine in the flooded room. Cindy and Nathan won't.

I pop my head above the surface as the blood gets thicker in the water. I can see the rocky wall just ahead of me. Almost there.

I dive back into the water and down to the ocean floor. A spear gun would have sunk to the bottom when Octo and the Guardians killed the men carrying them.

I haven't crossed over the reef yet into the human world. Those first two men had spear guns, maybe I can find one of them without having to go toward the beach with all the blood and bodies and probably sharks.

I see one of the guns laying in the sand ahead of me, but between me and it, sharks are swarming the bodies of the two men.

I watch the sharks as I swim closer. They're only paying attention to the bodies, not to me. They're tearing and ripping the men to pieces. Certainly, they'll just continue to eat what they have instead of coming after me, right?

I take a deep breath and steel myself. I'm just going to have to risk it and try to sneak by them as casually as possible. I'll try to stay away for as long as I can. I take another deep breath and swim as close to the reef as I can.

As I get closer to the shark frenzy, I'm relieved to see that most of the sharks are smaller, so they probably won't bother me.

There are a couple of very large ones though, and I just try to ignore that fact. I don't even look at them closely enough to figure out what type of shark they are. Knowing will only scare me. I just remind myself of what Octo taught me. That shark we encountered outside of our home was much bigger than these. I tell myself if that was fine, then this will be fine.

I slowly swim along the reef desperately trying not to draw attention to myself. I think I probably hold my breath the entire time I swim past them. Fortunately, none of the sharks take any notice of me, and I let out a sigh of relief.

I make it to the spear gun and grab it from the sand. It's then that I see that it doesn't have a spear. I want to scream in frustration, but instead I try to hold it all in. In my head though, I'm screaming, "Fuck! Fuck, Fuck, fuck!"

I look around trying to find one of the spears. I see a glint of metal directly under where the sharks are feeding on the body of one of the men.

My heart sinks. That's the worst place for it to be.

I take a deep breath again to prepare myself. Then I look at Xaiolpa and point to the spear underneath the sharks.

She gives me a frustrated, pitying look, and then quietly whispers, "It should be fine. Most of them are too small to attack us anyway. Plus, they already have food. You swim along the bottom and grab the spear. I'll stay above you and push back any sharks that show any interest in you."

I give her a terrified look. "Thank you."

She nods and uses her hand to motion me forward.

I swim so close to the bottom that my breasts and belly scrape against the sand. I take a deep breath when I get close to the body and hold it. I slowly make my way toward the spear, reaching my hand out as far as I can. When my fingertips touch metal, I grab it. I continue swimming forward underneath the sharks and body.

I'm nearly clear of the body when a small shark bumps into my leg. It bounces off and grazes along my butt as it swims away.

As I clear the sharks, I let out my held breath and take a deep breath of relief. I begin swimming back toward Xaiolpa. She makes a large circle around the sharks and meets me on the other side.

Her eyes are flashing with the excitement of it. "Did you get it?"

I nod enthusiastically. "Let's get back. We have to be fast."

She nods and we both take off swimming toward the facility.

I hold tight to the spear and the spear gun like my life depends on it. Not my life—Cindy's life, and I value her life far more than my own.

My pulse pounds in my ears again as I speed back to the facility. While I'm swimming, I wonder how high the water has gotten in the room. I wonder if they are having to float or if they can still stand on the floor. The thought of them treading water while they wait for me pushes me to swim faster.

By the time the facility is in sight, I can feel my legs burning from the exertion. I keep pushing though. I can't stop. Cindy needs me.

Once I'm close enough, I swim straight to the underwater window at the facility. Ovaggd'tho and Vrala are waiting for us. There were other Guardians with us earlier and I have no idea where they've gone, but I can't worry about that right now.

Panting, I say, "I got it." I hold up the gun and spear for them to see.

I finally risk a look in the room and see that it's half full. It's deeper than Nathan or Cindy can stand and Octo has tentacles wrapped around them, holding them up.

Fear sears through me. It's worse than I imagined. Cindy and Nathan look so helpless.

I put the end of the spear in the hole on the gun. I press the spear tip against the glass to push it in. Then once it clicks in place, I pull it away from the glass and I'm pleased to see that just loading it has cracked the surface of the window.

My plan is to get a few inches away from the window and shoot it point blank.

I get in position and motion for Octo to move them away from the window. He backs up to his tank inside. I nod to him.

Okay, the moment of truth. I take a deep breath and pull the trigger.

Chapter 27

Octhogh'xu / Octo

After what feels like ages, my Naomi returns to the window with one of the weapons that the humans shot at us. She presses the short spear against the glass to load it into the weapon.

While she was gone, the room filled with significantly more water. The water is well above the humans' heads, so I'm holding them in my tentacles to keep their heads out of the water. It is not a hardship for me, but I could tell that both of them were uncomfortable with my limbs on them.

Naomi backs away from the window just a little bit and motions for me to get back. I nod and move back as far as I can. Then I tell the humans to take a deep breath when she fires the weapon.

I see Naomi take a deep breath, then she fires it. Both humans suck in air as soon as they see the spear move.

The spear hits the glass hard. I can feel the vibrations of it through the water. It creates a small crack in the glass. I initially think it's just a superficial scratch, but then I see a small trickle of water leaking down the glass. It must have made a small hole!

This is good. We are weakening it!

Ovaggd'tho stabs the hole with his spear, and I see a few tiny cracks form. He stabs it twice more, but cracks are forming slowly. It would take a long time to get through the window this way.

I see Vrala say something to Ovaggd'tho and Naomi. They both nod to him and Naomi peers into the room with a worried look.

Everyone moves back away from the window while Vrala swims a small distance away from it.

I see him get in position to begin moving water. I say to the humans, "Be ready to take a deep breath and hold it. When the glass breaks, I'll quickly swim you to the surface."

I feel the force of the water as it begins to press on the glass. I can feel when Vrala increases it. I realize that the humans are looking at the window afraid, and they must not be able to feel what's happening.

To calm their fears, I say, "He's pushing water against the crack."

Their eyes get big. Cindy says, "He can manipulate water?"

I nod.

Vrala is pushing the water against the crack with a lot of force at this point, and the glass begins to crack again. It pops loudly with each crack.

I tell the humans, "Be ready." I see them taking deep breaths to prepare themselves.

With a loud splintering pop, the window splits in two. It feels like time pauses for a moment, then the glass shatters and water immediately floods in.

I hold the humans close to my body and feel them both grab onto me as I propel them out of the room and toward the surface.

I ignore everyone—including Naomi—to get them to air. Our heads break through the surface, and I hear both of them gasping in breaths.

Cindy starts to laugh. "Oh my gods, I can't believe that worked!" She looks around blinking at the bright sunlight.

Naomi's head breaks through the surface, as does Ovaggd'tho's and Xaiolpa's. Naomi immediately flings herself against me, wraps her arms around me, and kisses me.

I can see the tears in her eyes as she says, "Octo, you're safe! I was so afraid I would lose you! And thank you for saving them." My eye is riveted to her. My fierce, beautiful mate; I was so afraid that she would get hurt, but she saved me. I'm in awe of her.

She looks at Cindy, and Cindy says, "See? I told you we would get your tentacle guy back." They both laugh weakly at the joke.

We all turn to look at the building. The sight I'm faced with startles me. Four Guardians have climbed the embankment and are battling humans on the patio. Several humans lay dead on the ground, and others locked themselves inside the building.

Vrala calls out to the Guardians and they all jump back into the water. Then he unleashes wave after crashing wave onto the building.

We watch as all the windows break, and any humans that are not caught in the water are forced to run out of the front of the building.

Vrala continues to batter the building with water, breaking walls and twisting metal, forcing the humans further and further away from it.

Once he feels that the building is adequately destroyed, he swims back to us. The other Guardians also join us.

I look at each of them and say, "Thank you, brothers and sister, for your help today. I'm in debt to all of you."

They all nod.

Vrala says, "Call if you need help again. Hopefully they'll stay away for a while this time, but we will keep a close eye on this building." Then he nods, slips down into the water, and swims off.

The other Guardians say their goodbyes and swim away as well.

Naomi turns to Cindy. "Here, climb onto my back and we'll swim you down to one of the beaches closer to the hotel."

Cindy reaches over and grabs onto Naomi's shoulders, then loosely wraps her arms around Naomi's neck to hold on.

I continue holding onto the male as we begin swimming away from the facility.

The male clears his throat and says, "Thank you for helping us. We would have died back there."

I nod. "Thank you for helping me as well. I shudder to think of what would have happened to me in that building."

He furrows his brow, looking disturbed by the idea. He shakes his head to get rid of those thoughts then says, "By the way, my name is Nathan."

"My name is Octhogh'xu, but you can call me Octo. That's the name Naomi has given me, and I've become quite fond of it."

Nathan smiles at that. "Please take care of her and treat her well, Octo."

I give him a serious look. "I vow that I will."

He just nods.

I watch Naomi and Cindy as they swim. They're laughing and talking. I can see that they have been friends for a very long time and are very close.

Cindy giggles and says, "This reminds me of when we used to go swimming as kids and we carried each other around the pool."

Naomi laughs, "I was just thinking the same thing."

Cindy sobers a little. "Remember how you always wanted to be a mermaid? You always pretended to be one in the pool. Maybe it was some sort of intuition."

Naomi chuckles. "I doubt that. I don't think there's any way I could've had any type of intuition about all of this."

Cindy shrugs, still hanging onto Naomi's back. "You never know."

The females continue talking, but I don't really pay attention to what they're talking about.

We swim to one of the beaches that's close enough that Cindy and Nathan can walk to the place They're staying.

We swim over the protective reef, and up to the sandy beach. Once they're both safely able to stand, they climb off of me and Naomi.

Ovaggd'tho and Xaiolpa say their goodbyes. Cindy and Nathan thank them for all of their help, then Naomi gives Xaiolpa a tight hug.

After Ovaggd'tho and Xaiolpa leave, Cindy turns to Naomi and says, "Okay, now you have to tell me how this happened." Then she gestures between me and Naomi.

Naomi and I exchange a look.

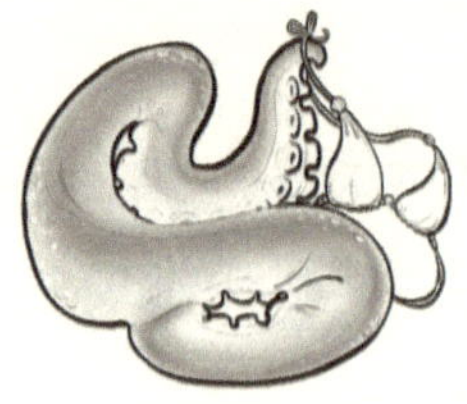

Chapter 28

I really don't want Cindy to hate Octo, but I don't know how to tell the story about how we ended up mated without telling her all of the bad parts. Maybe I can just omit some information.

I look at Cindy and say, "Well...it was the morning after I got here. I was really hungover from drinking the night before. I decided to come down to the beach and Octo 'scented' me. He knew I was his mate, that I was made for him. He came up on the beach and...well...we hit it off and...uh I became his mate." I laugh nervously, then just leave it at that.

Cindy just raises her eyebrows. "Naomi, do you seriously think I'm going to buy that bullshit? A tentacle guy—no offense—comes up on the beach and you just decide to turn yourself into a fish woman and live under the ocean with him?"

I cringe. "Well…"

Cindy sighs and rubs her forehead, "I'm guessing that I'm not going to like this story. So…out with it. Get it over with."

I sigh, then glance at Octo. He's looking down—probably in shame. "He grabbed me and dragged me into the ocean. Once we were underwater, he bit me. It was his mating bite. It did this to me." I gesture to myself with one hand. "I was unconscious and he took me to his home. When I woke up—well—to say I wasn't happy would be an understatement. I gave him hell and fought him and screamed at him. He had to lock me in a cage."

Cindy and Nathan are staring at me in astonishment. Cindy finally says, "How do you go from that to begging me to help you save your mate?"

I shrug. "I don't really know. He didn't hurt me even though I was cruel to him. He took care of me. And somewhere along the way, I started liking him and understanding him."

Cindy raises her eyebrows again. "Understanding him—Naomi—what? I mean, what the fuck? Seriously, Naomi, blink twice if you need help and I'll take care of this mother fucker."

I quickly say, "No, it's not...it's not like that. This is what his people do."

Cindy's voice gets a little shrill. "Steal women? Is that what you mean, because it sounds like that's what he did."

"No, I mean—their females want strong mates. So, when a male scents their mate, they claim her by stealing her and taking her back to their nest. The females are meant to fight. If he's able to best her and get her back to his nest, then she feels he's strong enough to be her mate."

I risk a glance at Octo. He has become very focused on a cut on his arm and isn't making eye contact with anyone.

I look back at Cindy, and she's giving me an exasperated look.

She huffs and says, "Naomi, that's fucked up. You know that's fucked up, right? I need to know that you know that's fucked up."

I sigh, "Yes, I know. Trust me I know."

Cindy sighs and stares at me. I don't know what else to say to her. Then she starts staring at Octo. He looks at me, not really sure how to handle this kind of scrutiny.

Finally, Cindy says, "Okay. Okay. You said you love him, right?"

I look Cindy straight in the eye and say, "Yes. I do love him." I glance over at Octo and he's watching me with a look of wonder on his face.

Then Cindy looks at Octo, "You love her, right? You'll take care of her? Treat her well? Keep her safe? Not lock her in a fucking cage?"

Octo is confident in his response, "Yes, I do love her. I'll take care of her, treat her well, and keep her safe. And not lock her in a cage. I vow this."

I can feel the prickle in my eyes and have to blink back tears. I know I must be grinning like an idiot now.

Cindy finally throws her hands up in the air. "Okay, well if you two are happy, then that's good enough for me. We will just call that first part weird cultural differences."

I laugh at that.

Cindy laughs with me and shakes her head. "So, what now?"

"I can't leave, Cindy. I live here with Octo now."

Cindy snorts. "Yeah, I noticed." She goes quiet for a minute and then says, "Well, we can come visit. Stay in the hotel and come down to the beach. We can see each other a few times a year that way."

I really do start crying now. "I would love that."

Cindy leans down to hug me, then she says, "You know...everything is still booked for the wedding. I haven't gotten any deposits back yet. What if Nathan and I have it on the beach, right in the water? You could watch from the water. The wedding party left days ago, so it would just be us. But I'm okay with that."

I start crying harder and a sob escapes me. "That would be perfect. Thank you, Cindy. I love you."

She hugs me tightly again. "I love you too, Naomi." We continue hugging, then after a minute or two, she adds, "Hey, bring your friends too."

I nod into her shoulder.

When we finally let go of each other, she says, "Well, it looks like we still have a wedding to get ready for, and I'm exhausted. I'll call and let the officiant know, then I'm going to take a shower and sleep. See you tomorrow? Same time as we originally planned?"

I smile, wiping tears away. "I wouldn't miss it."

Cindy and Nathan walk out of the water and up to the beach. They turn back and wave to us, then they make their way back to the hotel. I watch them as they go.

Chapter 29

As I'm watching them, I feel one of Octo's tentacles wrap around my calf. I turn to him and see that he has a worried look on his face.

"Naomi, are you well?"

I nod and fling myself into his arms, then I start sobbing. "I thought I lost you, Octo."

He strokes his hands up and down my back as he holds me. Then he buries his face in my neck. "Shhh, I'm fine."

We stay there holding each other for what feels like a long time. Finally, Octo says, "Come, let's go home. We can catch food on the way."

He takes my hand and we dive back into the water and swim back over the reef.

He gets out his net, and on the way home we catch crabs and urchin and then harvest some oysters. We take our time quietly hunting for our food. After such an eventful day, it feels so strange to be doing something as normal as gathering food.

A school of yellow fish swims by. They're the same fish that Xaiolpa was eating the other day. "Octo, can we catch some fish to eat too?"

He looks at me surprised. "Yes. I can catch fish for you."

He watches the school of fish as they circle back, and I watch as he goes still to prepare for them. As soon as they swim by, two of his tentacles lash out. They each grab a fish. He quickly grabs them with his hands and uses his claws to kill them.

I watch all of this in amazement. He was so fast. I don't see how I will ever be able to do that.

A group of large blue fish swims toward him, and I watch as he does the same thing again. He catches two blue fish this time. He puts the fish in the net, then looks at me and says, "Do you want more?"

I shake my head. "That will be enough for me to try it and see if I like it."

We continue gathering oysters, urchin, and crabs. Once the bag is full, we make our way, hand in hand, back to our home. When I see our wrecked ship in the distance, I feel such a relief. I really did not know if we would make it back here today.

I look at Octo and say, "Does this sort of thing happen a lot?"

He glances back at me. "What sort of thing?"

"The attack and battle on the beach."

He shakes his head. "No, that's not common at all. Hopefully we'll never have to deal with that again."

I breathe a sigh of relief. "Good."

He reluctantly adds, "Although, I'm worried they will come back."

I'm worried about that too, but I don't voice my concern. I don't want to stress him out.

Once we're inside our ship, we begin eating. We're quiet at first. I think we both have a lot to process from today.

Octo hands me one of the yellow fish. "Here, try this one."

I cautiously take it, and just look at it in my hand. "How do I take the insides out?"

He smiles, then takes the fish back. He shows me where to grab it and pulls the entrails out for me. Then he hands it back to me.

I stare at it in my hand. At least the guts are gone, but I still don't know if I can eat the scales and bones. Finally, I say, "In my world, we clean them first. They take the guts and bones out and then remove the scales."

He furrows his brow as I tell him this. "That's a lot of work for just one fish."

I shrug. "You should see how we eat crabs—we take the shells off first."

He looks aghast, and I laugh at the look on his face.

He shakes his head in disbelief. "Just bite it. Once you take the insides out, it is ready to eat. You don't need to do all that other work. Start with the tail."

I take a deep breath, then I bite the tail off the fish. It's strange and crunchy, but not terrible.

Octo watches me as I take another bite. This time I take a bite from along the back so that I'm getting the meat I would get if it were cleaned like normal. It has a very strong fish flavor, and it's not nearly as good as the crab. Plus, the bones and scales and head kind of freak me out. I finish chewing the bite in my mouth and look at the fish I'm holding. I don't think I can eat anymore of this. The idea of it makes my stomach roil, but I don't want to offend him.

Finally, Octo says, "Naomi, you don't have to eat it if you don't want to."

I let out a sigh of relief as he reaches toward me and takes the fish from my hand. He tosses the whole thing into his mouth and chews it up.

Quietly I say, "Sorry, I don't think I can eat the bones and head. Plus, I really love the flavor of the crabs."

We continue eating quietly. After a while, he says, "Thank you, Naomi, for fighting so hard to save me. I know that you're the reason that I'm here right now. My people wouldn't have known what to do to save me."

I smile and brush away the compliment. "You don't need to thank me. I'm your mate. I'm supposed to help you."

He grins at me. "I'm glad I chose a brave warrior female as a mate."

I just laugh, "Well, I'm not sure I'm a brave warrior—but thank you."

He gives me a surprised look. "You don't think you're a warrior?"

I shake my head. "You're my mate. I was just doing what I had to so I could get you back. And—I didn't feel like a brave warrior, I was terrified."

He watches me for a moment. "But, Naomi, that's what it is to be brave. You fight even though you're afraid."

I sigh, "I guess so. Although I didn't actually fight any-one."

Octo laughs deeply. "And do you think that you did not fight me when I took you?"

I smile to myself. "Okay, I did put up a fight then. But again, I was just doing what I had to."

Octo nods, "Of course. That's because you are a warrior." He gives me a devilish grin. "Once I teach you how to use a spear, you will be unstoppable."

I perk up at that. "You're going to teach me?"

He nods.

We continue eating our meal in comfortable silence. My mind wanders back to the events from today, and from seeing Cindy.

I'm so grateful that I was able to see Cindy and that she accepted me without too much grumbling. She gave Octo shit about kidnapping me, but—he deserved that. I've forgiven him for it, but that doesn't mean it's okay that he did it.

Once I finish my last crab, Octo cleans up from dinner, folds up his net, and slips it in his pouch. Then he looks me up and down and holds out his hand as he says, "Come, my fearless warrior female, let's go to our nest. I would like to show you just how proud I am of you."

I blush as I take his hand. "I like the sound of that."

As he pulls me against him, his tentacles wrap around me, holding me in his grasp. He kisses me deeply, then runs his mouth over my gills.

I sigh in pleasure as he kisses them, and gasp when he runs his tongue over them. They're so sensitive, easily as sensitive as my nipples.

I feel one of his tentacles nudge between my legs then slide through the folds of my pussy. I lean into him and wrap my arms around his neck as he continues to tease me.

He kisses me again. His tongue plunges into my mouth as he devours me. His tentacle begins pressing into my heat, and I whimper into his mouth.

I feel a second tentacle press into me, joining the first, and I moan. He begins thrusting them in and out of me, fucking me with them.

At the same time, he kisses down my neck and over my gills, causing me to shudder and whimper. He kisses his way down my chest and sucks one of my nipples into his mouth. My breath hitches as I feel his tongue flick over it.

His tentacles begin fucking me harder. I cry out on each thrust as it jolts my body in his grip.

Then I feel one nudge at my butt. He very gently works it into me. I moan as it works deeper into me. Somehow he manages to fuck me hard with the tentacles in my pussy while gently working the one in my butt. I feel so full and so overwhelmed by all of the sensation.

"Fuck...Octo." I moan again.

He licks my nipple one last time then palms my breast, pinching my nipple between his claws. He kisses me again, claiming my mouth and devouring me.

With his tentacles wrapped around me and inside me, I feel completely consumed by him. I'm weightless in the water and his grasp. His touch is all I feel, and it's everywhere.

Pleasure quickly builds inside of me; I feel like a fire has ignited in me and I'm just waiting to explode. I wrap my arms around his neck tightly, clawing into his shoulders and back.

I feel a tentacle lightly brush over my clit as the others thrust into me. My whole body quivers at that small touch and Octo swallows my moan.

His tentacle teases my clit again, and I whimper and tremble more. My heart is racing and I'm gasping for breath.

Then I feel a sucker work its way onto my clit and that fire inside of me explodes. I cry out as I come. My whole body shudders and seizes as wave after wave of pleasure rolls through me.

I'm gasping by the end of my orgasm and still clinging to Octo's neck. He slips his tentacles out of me and then presses me down onto his cock.

I moan loudly as his cock slides into me and fills me completely.

He turns us and presses my back against the wall of the ship as he slides his cock almost all the way out of me, then he swiftly thrusts it back into me. His tentacles latch onto the wall around me and he uses his claws to hold onto the wall on either side of my head. I feel like I'm completely enclosed by him as he continues to fuck me.

I moan with each thrust, and I can already feel that fire igniting inside of me again. He snakes one of his tentacles between us, and it lightly brushes against my clit. I gasp and buck my hips into his thrust.

His tentacle moves and presses against my clit, and my body quakes from the pleasure as I moan loudly.

Octo leans into me and licks along my gills as he works that tentacle and fucks me, and that fire inside me explodes again. I moan and gasp as I come. I writhe against him and feel my pussy pulse around his cock.

He snaps his hips against me, burying his cock inside me. Then he gasps and groans as he comes, pulse after pulse of seed spilling inside me.

We're both left breathless and gasping.

Octo kisses me, gently tangling his tongue with mine. Then his tentacles release from the wall. He wraps me in them and settles us in our nest to sleep.

I nuzzle my face into his neck. Just before I drift off to sleep, I say, "I love you, Octo."

He rubs his palm down my back, and I can feel the slight scrape of his claws as he says, "I love you too, Naomi."

Chapter 30

In the morning, I wake before Naomi. I watch her as she sleeps, and I silently thank the Gods of the Sea that she's my mate. I wasn't lying to her yesterday when I said that I wouldn't be here if it weren't for her. Because of her, my people were able to save me.

I was proud when I saw her alongside the other Guardians.

After a while, I gently wake Naomi. She wants to see Cindy be mated to Nathan and I'm curious about this also. My people don't have mating ceremonies, but I wonder if Naomi may want one. I'm planning to speak to Xaiolpa about it after we see what this ceremony is like.

Naomi stretches and groans, then snuggles back against me.

"Naomi, we must get up if you want to go to your friend's mating ceremony."

She stretches again, then says, "Can we tell Xaiolpa and Ovaggd'tho about it? Do we have time?"

"Yes. I think they would enjoy seeing the ceremony." I think for a moment, then add, "Well, Xaiolpa will probably enjoy it more than Ovaggd'tho."

Naomi smiles. "That's just like humans. Women usually enjoy weddings more than men."

Naomi rolls over onto my chest, then begins kissing me. In a husky voice she says, "Do we have time before we need to leave?" I can scent her arousal.

I feel my cock beginning to swell and preparing to extrude.

She reaches her hand down and behind my tentacles. She strokes her hand over my cock pocket and over the very tip of my cock. I groan from the pleasure, and she gasps and says, "Oh! Is that what it feels like before it's...out?"

I breathlessly say, "Yes."

"So, the tip of your cock doesn't go into the pouch, it stays poking out a little?"

I nod. This is both embarrassing and arousing.

She runs her hand over it again, and my cock forcibly extrudes from my cock pocket. She smiles and strokes her hand up it.

I wrap my fingers around her jaw and pull her face toward me to kiss her. Her kiss is gentle at first, then she opens for me and I delve my tongue into her mouth. I love the way she tastes.

She whimpers into my mouth as I run one of my tentacles along her sex. It's slick with her need, and I slip my tentacle inside her.

I enjoy listening to the sounds she makes as I thrust my tentacle into her. After the next thrust, I pull my tentacle all the way out of her, and she whimpers at the loss of it.

I grab her hips and shift her onto my cock. I gasp as her sex squeezes my cock tighter than I ever could have imagined. She moans once my cock is buried inside her.

She's wrapped in my tentacles and arms, and as I thrust into her, I slide a tentacle up to rub the nub that is so sensitive at the apex of her sex.

She moans. "Fuck...Octo."

I thrust harder into her. Her sex is squeezing me so tight that I groan. I feel like I could come at any moment. I rub my tentacle against her nub, enjoying how it makes her tremble and gasp. I move it so that a sucker grasps onto the sensitive spot. Naomi cries out loudly. I work all of the suckers on that tentacle and continue to thrust into her. Naomi's cries get louder, and her legs begin to tremble. Then she screams out as she comes. Her sex squeezes my cock, pushing me over the edge of my own orgasm. I groan as I come and fill her with my seed.

We're both clinging to each other and gasping by the time we're done.

Naomi kisses me deeply. Then we begin to untangle ourselves from each other.

She says, "I guess we should probably get Xaiolpa and Ovaggd'tho, so we can get to the beach in time for the wedding."

"Xaiolpa and Ovaggd'tho are actually coming here. They wanted to talk to me about the facility that we destroyed. They've heard from other Guardians that humans have been seen there again."

Naomi stills once I finish speaking. She gives me a worried look. "Are they coming back? Should we worry?"

I shake my head, "It's nothing like that yet. I think they've come back to assess the damage and to collect their dead."

She looks down at her hands. "Oh." She pauses for a minute or two, then says again, "Should we worry about them coming back?"

"Don't worry about that right now; only time will tell what the humans will do. We are safe here, that's what's important."

She nods, but I can tell she's still worrying about it. She says, "Should we catch some food? Do we have time to eat? I still don't know how to tell what time it is."

I glance out the broken windows and say, "It's still early morning. When was your friend planning to have her ceremony?"

"Late morning. So, we have time to eat. Thank the gods, because I feel like I'm starving today."

I look over at Naomi. Could she... "Naomi? How do humans have young?"

She gives me a startled look. "What do you mean, how do humans have young? We have sex...mating."

I shake my head, "No, I mean what type of young and how many do humans have? My people have hatchlings, and we have five to eight of them at once."

Her eyes go wide. "Oh. We usually have one, sometimes two, and very rarely three or more babies at a time. A woman carries a baby in her belly until it's born." Naomi pauses for a moment. When she starts talking again, her voice trembles a little. "You said hatchlings, do you mean eggs? Do your people lay eggs?"

But I'm lost in thought, live born young. That's certainly different than what my people do. I wonder how Naomi and I will have young, if we even can.

Naomi is giving me a worried look, and her voice is a little more shrill when she speaks. "Octo, you're freaking me out a little. Am I going to lay eggs?"

I snap out of my thoughts. "Well, my people lay eggs. The female carries them in her belly for about half of the incubation period, then they lay the eggs and the male helps protect and incubate the eggs until they hatch."

Naomi has a panicked look on her face. "Octo—am I going to lay eggs? Oh, my gods, it's not like we used condoms or any kind of birth control. Octo, what does this mean? Am I going to lay eggs like your people or give birth to a baby like a human? I'm not even human anymore. I'm like a fish lady or something—shit—I bet a fish lady would lay eggs."

Naomi is nearly hysterical. She rubs her hands down her face and is breathing hard, so I wrap my arms around her and say, "Shhh. I don't know Naomi. I don't know if we can even have young. And if we can, I don't know if it will be eggs or a baby."

Naomi starts to cry. "What are we supposed to do, just wait and see what happens?"

"No, there's a healer nearby. We can go to them. They should have answers for us."

Naomi sniffs and nods. "You think I'm pregnant, don't you? It's because I said I was hungry."

I shake my head. "I don't know what to think. I don't know if you could be pregnant. In my people, one of the first signs is that the female is very hungry. But you're not one of my people. You could just be hungry. We had a stressful day yesterday, and you swam a lot. We'll have to go to a healer to find out more. But don't worry Naomi."

She nods.

I hear the sound of someone clearing their throat and turn to see Xaiolpa and Ovaggd'tho waiting for us outside of the broken-out window.

Xaiolpa takes one look at Naomi and says, "Oh Naomi, are you well? Yesterday was a difficult day."

Naomi nods. "Yes, we were just..."

Naomi pauses. I can see Xaiolpa and Ovaggd'tho tense up. They likely think that we have been fighting. I notice Xaiolpa glance at the cage and I frown.

Naomi must see it too because she quickly adds, "We were just talking about...um...babies...or hatchlings, I guess."

Xaiolpa and Ovaggd'tho look relieved. Xaiolpa says, "Oh, well we wanted to wait a while to have hatchlings, so we went to a healer to delay it. I'm sure you can do the same if you aren't ready for them yet."

Naomi says, "It's not really that. It's that we don't know what kind of...um...young I would have. Or even if I could have young with Octo."

They look between both of us confused.

Naomi continues, "Humans carry babies in their bellies until they're born. Live birth. And we usually only have one at a time. But Octo says your people lay eggs and then guard them until they hatch. We don't know how it will work for me."

Xaiolpa and Ovaggd'tho both look surprised.

Xaiolpa says, "Oh, that is very different. But Naomi, I don't think you should be worried. Octhogh'xu's mating bite has made it so that you can live down here with him and be compatible with him. I'm certain it would have taken care of this part as well. You should see a healer, but it's nothing to worry over. Whichever way you bring the little ones into this world will be the right way for the two of you."

Naomi looks a little more relaxed. "I'm just afraid. Laying eggs sounds pretty terrifying."

Xaiolpa laughs, "I think birthing live young sounds far scarier."

Naomi chuckles at that. "That's true, all of the stories I've heard of childbirth seemed pretty terrifying."

I reach over and hug Naomi again. "Thank you for calming Naomi's fears, Xaiolpa."

Xaiolpa just smiles and nods.

To Naomi, I say, "We'll go see a healer tomorrow if you would like to."

She nods, still lost in thought. After a few minutes she seems more like herself. She gives Xaiolpa an excited look. "You're going to be so excited. Cindy and Nathan have decided to have their wedding ceremony today on the beach—basically in the water—so we can watch it too. She told me to invite you and Ovaggd'tho."

Xaiolpa claps her hands together. "Oh, that's wonderful! I would love to see a human mating ceremony."

I look at Naomi, "Do you want to go to the beach now? Are you still hungry?"

She says, "Let's go to the beach. I don't want to be late. I can grab a couple of crabs to eat while I swim, right?"

I nod.

She grabs my hand. "Let's go, then. I want to see Cindy."

Chapter 31

Octhogh'xu / Octo

We swim along the sea floor so Naomi and I can grab crabs as we go. I grab two and hand them to her. She takes a big hungry bite out of one, then quickly finishes it. She then starts eating the second one.

We're nearing the reef, and I grab two more. She takes them, eating them greedily.

"Do you want more, Naomi?"

She looks at the reef, judging how close we are to the beach. She shakes her head. "No, I think I'll wait until after the wedding."

Xaiolpa says, "Naomi, I can find an eel on the reef! They're delicious, I'm certain you'll love it."

Naomi grimaces a little and glances at me. I say, "I don't think she'll like it. She tried a fish recently, and...she didn't enjoy it very much. I imagine an eel would be worse than a fish."

Xaiolpa looks surprised.

Naomi says, "Humans eat fish differently. We clean all the guts and bones out of them. I had a hard time eating it with the bones still in there."

Xaiolpa gives me a wide-eyed look. "That must be a lot of work for just a little bit of food." She pauses to think about it, then continues, "In that case, I agree, an eel would be a terrible idea."

Naomi smiles warmly at her. "I think I'll just stick to crab for right now."

Once we're at the reef, Ovaggd'tho and I peer over it and make sure there aren't any other humans waiting for us.

There's no one in the water today, so I check above the surface and see several people on the beach. One of them is wearing all white. When I look more closely, I realize that it's Cindy.

Ovaggd'tho and I dive back down to our mates.

I swim up to Naomi and say, "No one is in the water today, but I see a few people on the beach. I think one of them is Cindy. She's dressed in all white."

Naomi's face lights up. "Yes! That's her."

We swim over the reef and toward the beach in front of the hotel.

Naomi says, "I'm going to look above to see what's going on." Then she sticks her head above water.

When she comes back under, she says, "It's Nathan, Cindy, and the wedding officiant. They're getting into place now. The officiant is out in the water with his back to us so he won't be able to see us. We should be able to keep our heads above water to watch."

The four of us stick our heads above water. It's just as Naomi described. The male that seems to be in charge of the wedding, has waded out into the water to about knee deep. He has his back to us. Cindy and Nathan are also in the water, but they are in water that is shallower and closer to dry land than the other man. They're facing each other, and Cindy holds something in her hands.

The male with his back to us begins speaking, "We have gathered here today to celebrate the joining of two souls in a lifelong commitment of love and devotion. It is a beautiful thing when two hearts find each other and commit to love and to care for each other through all of life's ups and downs."

I look at Naomi as she watches her friends, and she looks completely happy. She's smiling as she watches them. I wonder if she would want a human ceremony like this.

I return to listening to the wedding. The male is now saying, "Cindy and Nathan will now exchange rings as a symbol of their love and commitment to one another."

Nathan holds out his hand toward Cindy, and Cindy slides a ring onto his finger as she says a vow to Nathan. Then, Cindy holds out her hand to Nathan. He slides a ring onto her finger as he says a vow.

I look at my own hand. Even though it's just below the surface of the water, I can clearly see the webbing. I remember the webbing on Naomi's hand too. We couldn't wear rings like humans do. But I still wonder if Naomi would like some sort of token of our mating.

When I look back at Cindy and Nathan, the man is speaking again. "By the authority vested in me, I now pronounce you husband and wife. You may now kiss!"

Cindy and Nathan embrace and then kiss. You can clearly see how much they care for each other.

I look back at Naomi, and she has her hands clasped at her mouth. I'm dismayed to see tears streaking down her cheeks.

Slightly panicked I say, "Naomi, what's wrong?"

She wipes her eyes. "Lots of people cry at weddings. They're happy tears. I'm so happy for them, and I'm just so glad that I got to see this."

I look over and see that Xaiolpa is leaning against Ovaggd'tho. He has his arms around her, and she dabs at her cheeks as if she's wiping tears off her face too. She gives me a shy smile when she sees me looking at her.

I look back toward the beach, and the male in charge of the ceremony has walked off, and just Cindy and Nathan are left.

Naomi surges toward the beach and Cindy leans down to meet her in a tight hug. I follow Naomi and stay beside her.

As she hugs Cindy, I hear her say, "I'm so happy for you! Thank you for doing this so I could watch. I love you."

I can see tears run down Cindy's cheeks as she says, "I love you too, Naomi." She's quiet for a minute, then says, "I'm pretty sure that officiant thought I was crazy making him stand out in the water like that."

Naomi sniffs and laughs weakly.

They eventually pull themselves away from each other. Naomi looks at Cindy and says, "What are you going to do now?"

Cindy says, "We're going to take today and tomorrow as an actual honeymoon, then we're going home." Cindy looks back at Nathan as she says this. "We've stayed here a long time now, and it's time to get back home and back to work."

Naomi nods.

They're both silent for a moment, just watching each other. Cindy finally breaks the silence, "I don't know what I'm going to do without you around. I won't be able to text you or talk to you." Fresh tears roll down her cheeks.

Naomi hugs her again. I can hear her sniffle, and her voice sounds thick with tears. "I know. I'll be here though. You can come visit and catch me up on everything."

Cindy nods. "How will I let you know when I'm here? Put a note in a bottle and throw it over the reef?" She laughs.

Naomi chuckles. "Maybe." Then she looks at me.

I say, "I patrol the borders every day. If you come down to the beach, I'll see you. Or you could write Naomi's name in the sand."

Cindy's face lights up a little with that. "That's a good idea. We could write your name in the wet sand, or maybe I can get a banner made and bring it out here. They'll just think I'm mourning a lost friend."

Naomi smiles. "I like that idea."

They hug again, then Naomi says, "Go spend some time with your new hubby."

Cindy smiles and looks back at Nathan. When she turns back to Naomi, she says, "I'll come down to the beach to say goodbye on the day after tomorrow. Around noon. Sound good?"

"Sounds perfect. I'll be here."

They hug one last time and Cindy walks back to Nathan and takes his hand. Naomi wipes her eyes and looks at me. I tentatively take her hand.

I'm painfully aware that these two close friends are having to say goodbye to each other because of me. "Naomi...I'm sorry for tearing you and Cindy apart."

A tear escapes her eye and rolls down her cheek. She absently wipes it away. "It's okay. Honestly, I was afraid it was going to change anyway. Cindy and Nathan are married now, and I'm sure they will have a baby sooner rather than later. Before you grabbed me, I was single. I was secretly worried that I wouldn't fit into their world anymore."

I wrap my arms around her in a hug, and she hugs me back laying her head against my chest.

She sniffs again, and I suspect she's crying again. "My family life was horrible when I was a kid. Cindy has been my family for so long. I was afraid of what would happen when she got married and started her own family. But now I'm not afraid. For the first time in a long time, I feel like I belong...like I have my own family now...with you."

I squeeze her tighter as she says that. "You are everything to me, Naomi."

She looks up at me, and I lean down to kiss her. Once we kiss, she says, "Let's go home."

We both turn and swim back to Xaiolpa and Ovaggd'tho. They join us and we all swim back over the reef toward our home.

***

After we eat, Naomi and I mate again that night, and as she falls asleep entwined in my tentacles, I think about the ceremony from today.

I would like Naomi to have a mating ceremony. I could tell from today's ceremony that it's important to her people.

I could ask Xaiolpa to help me plan it, and Vrala could act as the man that's in charge of performing the ceremony. We can't do rings, but I could have a necklace made for her. I try to think about what I could turn into a necklace that would be special.

Then it hits me. The pearl.

I threw it down during our first meal. I try to sit up without disturbing Naomi. That day, I fed her through the bars, so it should be on the ground nearby. I'm able to sit up enough that I can just see the edge of the cage. That should be close enough. I scan the ground around it.

My eyes land on a faint shimmer of something lodged between two boards. That has to be it.

I stretch one of my tentacles out. If I stretch it as far as I can, I may be able to grab the pearl. I continue slowly stretching my tentacle. Once my tentacle is nearly stretched to its maximum length, I finally feel the edge of one of the boards that the pearl is stuck between. I pat around the board with the tip of my tentacle and try to position one of the suckers over the pearl.

It takes a few minutes of groping around before my sucker grabs the pearl and holds onto it. As I pull my tentacle back in, I curl it around the pearl so I don't accidentally drop it. Once my tentacle gets back to me, I drop it in my hand and then put it in the pouch that holds my net. I'll have to remember to be careful taking my net out tomorrow.

Tomorrow I'm going to take Naomi to the nearby underwater city of Cthegril to see a healer so we can find out what kind of young we can have.

I plan to wake Naomi up early and go to Ovaggd'tho's and Xaiolpa's home so I can ask Ovaggd'tho to check on the beach for me. Maybe I can pull Xaiolpa aside and ask her about planning a wedding, and the necklace.

My people get spears and metal things made by land dwelling Guardians and Elven. We trade for them. So, I should be able to have the pearl made into a necklace for Naomi; I'll just need an excuse to leave Naomi with Xaiolpa for one day. Maybe I can have Ovaggd'tho watch my territory again for that day while I go to one of the metalsmiths.

With a plan in mind, I curl up next to Naomi and sink into a restful sleep.

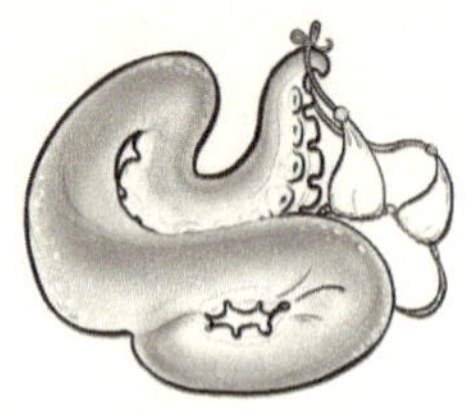

Chapter 32

Octo wakes me up early the next morning. The water still looks dark.

I rub my face as I wake up. "Are we up earlier than normal?"

He's getting his spear ready. "Yes, we're going to swim to Cthegril to see a healer so we can find out if you will lay eggs or give live birth."

"Oh." I'm suddenly really nervous about it. I'm honestly terrified of both answers. The idea of giving birth has always terrified me because of the pain and danger of it. Now I have a new reason to be afraid. I don't even have a concept of what it will be like to lay an egg. I'm guessing it's not a hard-shelled egg like a chicken. It's probably more of a squishy, jelly kind. If that's the case, then maybe it would be less painful than childbirth. Laying an egg would be weird, but less pain would definitely be a bonus.

I'm quietly thinking over all of this, when Octo says, "First we'll swim to Ovaggd'tho's and Xaiolpa's home so I can ask Ovaggd'tho to check on the beach for me today. Then we'll swim to the city."

Wait...a city? "Cthegril is a city? Like an underwater city?"

Octo nods.

That wakes me up. An underwater city! That sounds so magical.

I look at Octo excitedly. "Tell me about the city."

He shrugs. "It's just a city."

I roll my eyes and scoff. "It's not *just* a city. It's an underwater city. That's pretty amazing."

Octo gives me a look that says he doesn't think so.

"Seriously, Octo?! I've never seen an underwater city. Humans can't build cities under the ocean. So, to me it's really amazing."

He looks at me thoughtfully, "Well, I prefer it out here on my territory. There are too many people in the city."

"What kind of people, Guardians like you?"

He shakes his head. "Most Guardians like me have territories to protect. There are some Guardians that live there, but most of the people are Merfolk."

I gasp. "Like mermaids?"

He says, "Yes, like mermaids."

"Oh, my gods, mermaids are real! Humans were so certain that they were just made up."

He chuckles, "You have seen me, and yet you are surprised that mermaids exist?"

I just laugh, "Fair point." I quietly think for a moment. "You know, when I was a kid, all I wanted was to be a mermaid. I was obsessed with them." I sigh sadly, "Most of the other kids made fun of me for it. My mom made fun of me for it too." I glance at Octo, then add, "My mom was pretty mean to me. Cindy was the only one that didn't laugh at me about it."

I get quiet, and Octo studies me.

Finally, he says, "Your mother was cruel to you?"

I nod.

He furrows his brow. "What about your father, why did he allow this?"

I sigh, "He left when I was still a baby."

Octo gives me a confused look. "Your father left you? Why would he do that?"

I shrug. "He didn't want kids. My mom didn't either. I was an accident. He stayed until after I was born, but I guess a baby was too much for him. He left my mom and I when I was just a few months old. I think my mom always blamed me for it. That's why she was so mean to me. And then on top of being the child that she never really wanted, I was the weird kid, and the fat kid." I look down and rub a hand across my belly and then cross my arms to hide it.

I look at Octo, and he looks horrified. So, I say, "I guess fathers don't leave their children in your world?"

He looks shocked that I'm even asking that. "No. Fathers are honored to have young. And mothers aren't cruel to their young. They cherish them."

"Well...that's good. A lot of fathers abandon their women and children in my world. And a lot of mothers are disappointed in their children and cruel to them. It can make life hard for kids."

Octo comes over to me and strokes my hair. "I'm sorry you went through that, Naomi. Know this, I would never abandon you or our child."

I smile at that. "Thank you for saying that. I wasn't really worried, but I like hearing it. It's reassuring." I study his face for a minute, then add, "And I would never be cruel to our children. Children are precious, and they should be loved."

He smiles at me, then says, "Are you hungry today? Do you want to grab a few crabs while we swim over to see Ovaggd'tho and Xaiolpa?"

"Yes! I'm starving again just like I was yesterday."

Octo gives me a thoughtful look, with his spear in one hand, he reaches his other hand out to me. "Come, let's go."

We make our way to Ovaggd'tho's and Xaiolpa's cave, swimming along the ocean bottom. I grab a couple of crabs as we go.

When we get there, Octo speaks with Ovaggd'tho while Xaiolpa swims over to me to greet me.

She says, "I heard Octo say that you're going to the city to see a healer. That's exciting."

I give her a worried look. "I'm nervous about what they'll say."

Xaiolpa rubs my arm with her hand, "It will be okay no matter what they say. I'll be here to help you when the time comes no matter what."

I give her a quick hug. "Thank you, Xaiolpa."

Octo and Ovaggd'tho are still speaking, but they're looking at us now. They nod to each other and then Octo swims back to me.

He reaches for my hand and says, "Are you ready, Naomi?"

I nod nervously.

We say our goodbyes, and swim away from their cave.

After we've been swimming for a few minutes, I ask, "How long will it take us to get there?"

He says, "We should be there by around lunch time."

I raise my eyebrows at that. "It's pretty far then."

"It is not too bad. Don't worry, Naomi."

I nod, then we continue quietly swimming.

Chapter 33

Naomi

It turns out that *not too bad* for Octo, is way too much for me. It doesn't take me long to get tired from swimming. By the halfway point, I'm exhausted.

We stop to rest, and Octo grabs some oysters for me, which I greedily devour. I'm still exhausted, even after resting, so Octo decides to carry me the rest of the way.

The second half of the trip goes by a lot faster. I'm pretty sure he was swimming really slow in the beginning to help accommodate me.

When we get close, he points into the distance in front of us. "Look, Naomi. That's the city."

All I can see right now are dark shapes that resemble tall buildings in the distance. It makes me wonder if they have some way to build underwater buildings here.

As we get closer, I see that they are buildings that look like stacks of bubbles. I have no idea what the bubbles are made of though. Obviously, they aren't real bubbles. It almost looks like quartz, but how would they make whole buildings out of quartz?

As we get even closer, I see that each bubble appears to be living quarters like an apartment. There are beautiful green kelps, bright seaweeds, and even colorful corals growing in the crevices between the bubbles.

The bubbles seem to glow from lights within them.

It's beautiful. Everywhere I look, there are large clusters of tall, bubble buildings.

I gasp as I take it all in. "Octo, it's gorgeous! What are the buildings made of?"

"Some type of crystal. The Merfolk work with the Elven that live on land to build these. Some of the Elven family lines have magic that controls crystal like this, so they shape it into the buildings for the Merfolk. Before that, everyone lived in caves or shipwrecks like the rest of us."

And the people...they're everywhere. They swim between bubble buildings and stop to talk to each other. It's just like Octo said, they're Merfolk. They're literally mermaids...well, the females are. I guess the males would be mermen. They're a variety of vibrant colors like tropical fish. They have long tails with large, frilled tail fins. Their colorful scales cover their tails, then the scales run all the way up their torsos, fading out at their chests. The males have scales on their pectorals, but the females have visible breasts very similar to humans. They also have large, frilled dorsal fins. Their gills seem to be like mine; they have a small set along the sides of their throat, but unlike me, they also have a larger set that runs along their ribs. The skin on their upper bodies is colored to match the scales on their tales. Their hands have long, wicked-looking claws and webbing between their fingers—a lot like Octo's hands. They all have various shades of long hair that billows around their heads like mine does. One smiles at us as she swims by, and I see that they also have sharp teeth.

They're both beautiful and terrifying, because I know they must be incredibly strong and deadly.

Octo is still carrying me as we make our way through some of the bubble buildings. I'm staring at everything in wonder.

The fact that their gills are different than mine seems odd to me. Do they need that much more air than I do? "Octo...why don't I have gills on my sides like them? My neck gills seem to be the same, but I'm missing the big gills on my ribs."

He looks at them swimming around. "That's because you're more like me than like them."

I give him a confused look. "What do you mean?

"Your skin is like mine, and you don't have scales. You have a small set of gills like I do because your skin breathes too."

I suck in a breath. "Wait—what? My skin breathes?"

He chuckles. "Yes."

I stare at him wide-eyed. "But...wait...you said a small set of gills like yours. Where are your gills?" I lean into him to look at his neck.

He laughs again and shakes his head. "Here." He points to his bulbous octopus type mantle.

When I look up at where he's pointing, I see them moving with each breath. "Oh...I'd never noticed them." I feel slightly guilty as I admit that.

He raises his eyebrows and gives me an aghast look. "You did not know how your mate breathes?"

I grimace. I can't tell if I've legitimately hurt his feelings or not. I decide to keep it lighthearted just in case. "Well...I mean...I trusted that you were breathing. You're alive, after all."

He gives me an unimpressed look.

"Hey, it's been a lot for me to adjust to. Obviously, I didn't even know how I was breathing. I didn't know about the skin thing. I don't know how you can expect me to have known how you breathe..."

He chuckles and gives me a smile, then he says, "Let's go to the healer."

He continues to carry me into the midst of the bubble buildings as I look at everything, in complete awe of what I'm seeing.

Suddenly a thought occurs to me. "Octo, you said that this world is divided into Guardians and Elven, but you didn't say anything about Merfolk. Where do they fit in?"

He's quiet for a minute while he thinks. "Merfolk are more like the Elven than Guardians. They have no ties to land or territory like Guardians do. They don't have mating bites. They even look more like Elven—they just have fish tails instead of legs. I usually just think of them as the Elven of the Water."

"Okay, well I guess that makes sense."

He shrugs. "Like the Elven, they also tend to think that they're better than Guardians. Guardians tend to keep to their own instead of spending a lot of time around the Merfolk or Elven. At least my kind do."

"Will I ever see other types of Guardians?" I ask.

"Maybe. We would have to travel to see them. Most of the Guardians near my territory are like me, Ovaggd'tho, and Xaiolpa, but we do run into Guardians that look different occasionally."

I go back to quietly looking around. I'm trying to take everything in. It's all so beautiful and overwhelming.

I'm looking at the bubble buildings, admiring how they glow, when I suddenly realize that they must have some kind of lights in there.

"Octo, how are there lights inside the bubbles?" I point to the nearest one that's glowing.

He looks over at the one that I'm pointing to. "They have magical lights."

"What?! Really?"

He nods. "It's a type of spell that creates little glowing orbs."

I look at him shocked. "You say that as if it's nothing. Someone here can do magic that creates little glowing orbs? That's pretty amazing!"

He shrugs, then sighs when he looks at me. "It's Merfolk stuff. They like magic and pretty things. Guardians like me don't have much use for it. The only magic I worry about is the magic to call for help while I'm protecting my territory, and the powerful water magic that Vrala uses."

I keep watching him. There's obviously a lot of division between the Merfolk and his people. And I'm guessing between the Elven and his people too.

He adds, "I also care about the healing magic that can help my mate."

That catches my attention. "The healer is one of the Merfolk?"

Octo nods. "All of the healers I've ever met were Merfolk. I've never met a Guardian healer."

"Are all of the Merfolk able to heal?"

Octo shakes his head. "No, magical abilities vary from person to person among the Merfolk and Elven. Some don't have any magical abilities. Some have mild abilities, and others have very strong magical abilities. The ones with strong magical abilities are usually in charge of everything though."

"That makes sense."

Octo gives me a serious look. "We come to the healers as needed, and we buy and trade with everyone; however, Guardians keep their distance from the Elven and Merfolk. There is a lot of corruption in their worlds. It's best to stay clear of it."

I furrow my brow. Then I ask, "Is this dangerous...going to a healer? Are we in danger?"

He shakes his head. "No. It would only be dangerous for us if we got involved in their society."

I think about everything he's said. "So basically, we just need to just be outsiders."

He nods.

Octo stops at one of the bubble buildings and looks up. He points to a bubble and says, "The healer is the third one up there."

He sets me down and we both swim up to the bubble he pointed at. It has a door that looks like it's made from woven kelp. Octo knocks on the stone beside the woven door.

A female voice calls, "Just a minute."

We wait a couple of minutes at the door. Octo uses his tentacles to hold onto the side of the bubble. I just float and tread water when I need to. I suddenly realize that I can hear some sort of groaning noise coming from inside. Then there's a loud yell.

I look at Octo nervously and whisper, "What was that?"

He just shrugs. But he doesn't seem worried about it.

I hear the woman's voice again as she comes to the door. It sounds like she's admonishing someone. She has her head turned looking at someone inside the room as she opens the door. She says, "Hush now. You will be okay. You've had worse breaks than this one." I hear another groan from inside.

She's a bright yellow mermaid with some light orange striping on her fins. Her hair is light orange as well.

She turns and looks at us brightly. "Hello! How can I help you?" Her eyes land on me and she gasps. "Oh my, aren't you lovely! I haven't seen a Guardian take a human mate in a very long time. Come in, both of you." She waves us inside.

I look at Octo and he nods, then follows me in.

The bubble is actually far more spacious than I thought it would be. There are woven hammocks lined up in two rows in the room. The hammocks hook onto crystal bars that come out of the floor.

In the second row of hammocks, there's a merman occupying the one at the end of the row. His arm is in a woven sling and he winces in pain frequently. I notice his eyes lock on me as the healer brings us in.

The healer motions to the nearest hammock and tells me to sit.

I sit down on it and look up at her.

She looks at Octo and says, "I assume you two are here because of her. Or are you injured?"

Octo replies, "I'm fine. Yes, it's for her. We are recently mated and had some questions."

She nods. "I imagine you do." She looks at me and says, "Do you mind if I look over you to make sure the mating bite did everything it should?"

I nod.

She takes my hands one at a time and inspects the webbing between each finger. She then does the same with each of my feet. I'm usually quite ticklish on my feet, but I'm so nervous that it doesn't affect me at all this time. After checking them, she moves my hair and thoroughly inspects my gills. Once she's done with my gills, she looks in my mouth and then at my eyes.

I stare into her eyes as she studies mine. Her eyes are large and mostly black. It looks like her eye is mostly pupil, without the colored irises that humans have. And her pupils are huge. They're far larger than a human's pupils could ever get. It gives the appearance that her eyes are totally black, but when I look closely I can see a hint of white around the edges.

She nods once she's done. "Everything looks perfect. She should not have any problems."

I give her a small smile. "Thank you."

Octo says, "We were wanting to know—ah...humans give live birth, but my people's females lay eggs. Do you know...can we even have young together? If we can, will it be a live birth or eggs?"

I glance over at the merman in the other hammock. He's intently watching our conversation. I notice that he has the same large black eyes that the healer has.

The healer looks at me. "Can you please lie down?"

I nod and lie down on the hammock. It's actually far more comfortable than I thought it would be.

She feels on my stomach and presses in spots low on my belly. As she examines my belly, I give Octo a nervous look. He gives me a small smile of encouragement.

The healer then says, "If you don't mind, I would like to examine your breasts."

I subconsciously cover them with my arm and glance at Octo again, but he's still smiling and doesn't seem concerned. I slowly uncover them, and quietly say, "That's fine."

She has me raise each of my arms as she checks each of my breasts. It's actually pretty much the same thing my doctor does at my annual checkup, and that helps me relax just a little.

The healer then smiles at me. "You can sit up now." Once I sit up, she continues, "Well, you will have no problem having young—she's already pregnant."

I look at Octo and he has a huge smile on his face. I can tell this is what he wanted. I smile back at him even though I'm still nervous.

The healer continues, "It looks to me like she will have eggs like your people. Actually, just one egg. It's a bit larger than eggs normally are in your females, but that's just due to her being human before your mating bite."

I look at the healer and say, "So, it's just one baby?"

She nods.

Then I ask, "So, how long will the pregnancy be? Or well, how long until I lay the egg? Then how long until it hatches?"

The healer gives me a soft smile. "That part I cannot easily answer. I think it will be unique to the two of you. The females of his people typically take eighteen months to hatch the egg."

I gasp when she says that.

She laughs. "About nine months of that time is spent with the egg growing inside the mother. Then she lays the egg and it incubates for about another nine months before it hatches. But human gestation is complete in about nine months. I suspect you will have a much shorter pregnancy than what his people are used to, although it will probably be longer than what you're used to."

I take a deep breath and let it out. Then I nod. "Okay, I can handle that. Is there anything I should know about laying an egg? Will it be like childbirth?"

She laughs again. "No, it will be much easier than a human childbirth. You'll know when it is time to lay the egg. You'll have something similar to contractions that human mothers have, but not nearly as painful, and you will feel like you need to push. Be sure to get to your nest when you start having those contractions and just push when your body tells you to."

I nod, then look down and rub my stomach nervously.

She touches my shoulder. "There's no need to be nervous. There should be no complications. Do you happen to have a female that can come help you when the time comes?"

I smile and nod. "Yes, I have a neighbor that I have gotten to be close friends with. She's already told me she would help no matter what kind of birth I have."

The healer says, "Good. You will do fine. Do either of you have any other questions?"

I shake my head and look at Octo. He's shaking his head too, and he answers her. "I think that's all we needed to know, thank you, healer."

I stand up from the hammock, and she smiles at us brightly. "You're very welcome. And congratulations to both of you."

We are turning to leave when the merman in the back of the room says, "Excuse me."

Octo and I both turn to look at him. Octo positions himself slightly in front of me so that he's between me and the other male.

The merman continues, "I'm sorry, I couldn't help but overhear you. Did you say that she was human and then you gave her your mating bite?"

Octo gruffly says, "Yes."

"And it made those changes to her, and she can now live underwater with you?" he asks.

Again, Octo says, "Yes."

"How long did it take for her gills to form, did she need to stay out of the water for a while?"

Oct gives him a wary look. "No, they formed immediately after my bite. She was still for a moment and then she took her first underwater breath."

The merman nods to himself, clearly thinking about something. Then he says, "Thank you for answering my questions. And did I hear that she's expecting young?"

Octo nods.

The merman smiles. "Congratulations to you both."

Octo nods in return. I say, "Thank you. I hope you feel better soon."

The merman huffs slightly. "Me too."

The healer smiles. "Come, let's get you on your way." She leads us out the door. As we swim out, she says, "If you feel you need to see me again, don't hesitate to come."

We both thank her and Octo hands her a few coins. Then we swim back down to the ocean floor.

I look at Octo, and he's smiling back at me. I whisper, "We are going to have a baby." Then I wrap my arms around his neck and kiss him.

After we kiss, he picks me back up in his arms and turns to head out of the city.

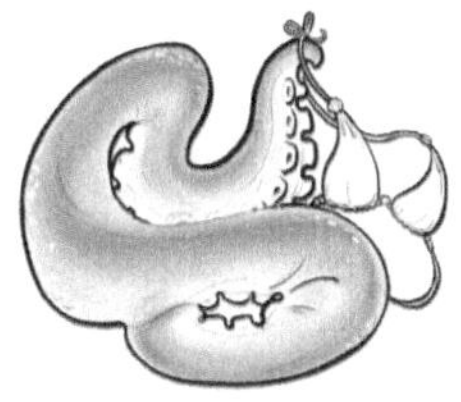

Chapter 34

Naomi

About halfway back to our nest, Octo changes directions and swims further out into the ocean.

"Are we going a different way?"

He nods, "Yes, there's something I want to show you."

As he swims, I notice that the water is getting colder and dimmer. We must be going deeper. Didn't he say that there were things that were dangerous in the deep waters? My stomach flips at the thought of something large and dangerous being out here with us.

"Hey, Octo, are we going deeper?"

He nods again.

"Um...didn't you say that there were things out there that could hurt us? Is it smart to go deeper?"

He smiles at me. "Don't worry, Naomi, I wouldn't put you in danger. We have to go deeper to see what I want you to see, but we are still safe."

I nod even though I'm still scared. I hug my arms a little tighter around his neck. Octo wouldn't let me get hurt.

We swim up to the top of a ridge and there's a sharp drop-off into deeper, darker water. I gasp when I look out at what's before us. I climb out of Octo's grip so I can swim a tiny bit closer to the edge.

In the middle of the darkness, I see small glowing shapes floating all around. They gracefully dance through the water. Jellyfish! There must be hundreds, maybe even thousands of them. As they cluster together, they look like glowing clouds floating through water. Below them, something much larger is glowing. As my eyes adjust, I see that it's bones. Massive bones that are glowing from deep within their marrow. I look out over all the bumps and ridges of the giant vertebrae that form the graceful line of a giant spine. Huge rib bones jut from the sand. There are large bones that may have once been flippers. Finally, I realize there is a massive skull. I've never seen a skull so large, and I'm not certain what type of animal it belonged to. The skull is long and oddly split and pointed at the mouth. It's a massive skeleton. My gaze sweeps over the larger area, and I realize there are more skeletons, dozens more. The quiet, peaceful glow goes on as far as I can see.

As I stare out across the ocean floor in wonder, I say, "Octo, what is this?"

"It's a whale graveyard."

"Gods, Octo, it's beautiful. Is that a swarm of jellyfish floating around them?"

"Yes, when the bones glow, it attracts jellyfish, and the jellyfish swarm thinking to find a mate." Octo explains.

"The bones don't always glow?" I ask.

Octo shakes his head, "No."

I look at him, "Can we go down there?"

He shakes his head again, "No. It's too deep and too cold. It's also a sacred place for many underwater people, mine included."

I give him a surprised look. This is the first time he's mentioned anything spiritual. "It's sacred? How?"

Octo exhales like he's nervous. "It is a place of great magic and power. These whales are the largest and strongest of all sea creatures, but they're also the gentlest. Their spirits are pure and made of strength and love. When they make their last voyage here for their final resting place, their spirits are set free. They're so pure that the gods of the sea turn them into the ocean itself. It is said that if you bring your mate here while they have young inside them, and the bones glow, then the gods will bless your young with strength and a good heart."

I swim back to him and hug my arms around his neck. "So, you brought me here so that our child could be blessed?"

He nods sheepishly. "I hoped the gods would bless us, but I was afraid…"

He trails off, and I hug him tight. "Thank you, Octo, for doing something so special for the baby. And it's beautiful. I'm glad I got to see it."

He smiles at me, and I watch his face as he looks out over the bones. He's in awe of it just like I am, but there's more there. Relief. He's relieved that the gods gave our child their blessing.

We float there looking out over the glow of the grave-yard. I can't deny that there's something powerful about this place. It feels sacred.

After a while, I finally speak. "I never really believed in the gods of my people. But this feels right. Maybe I was always meant to be here instead."

Octo says, "You were always meant for me, my mate."

When we're ready to leave, Octo scoops me up and carries me for the rest of the swim home. I'm exhausted, so I sleep in his arms for most of it.

When I wake up, Octo says, "Are you hungry? Do you want me to grab you some oysters or crabs? I can get some urchins from the kelp."

I shake my head and nuzzle my face back into his neck.

With a muffled voice, I ask, "How close are we to home?"

"We're almost there."

I look at him, "When we get home will you have to go out and patrol your territory?"

He shakes his head. "No, Ovaggd'tho has been patrolling it along with his territory. He'll stop by and update me before he goes home this evening."

I nod and lay my head back against him. We're quiet for a bit, then I ask, "Octo, are you excited about the baby?"

He hugs me tighter to his chest. "Yes, it's all I have ever wanted."

***

I sleep the rest of the way home.

Octo wakes me up when we're close. "Naomi, let's gather some food for dinner."

I yawn. "Okay."

When I look around, I realize that I can see our sunken ship in the distance.

Octo gets his net out, and we both swim around, gathering crabs and oysters. I find a few sea urchins too. Once the bag is full, we swim toward our nest.

As we are swimming, Octo stops at a cluster of small jellyfish. This kind doesn't have the long tentacles hanging off of them.

He grabs one and hands it to me.

"You can eat these too. They don't sting." He grabs another one and puts the whole thing in his mouth.

I watch him as he chews.

He looks at me and says, "Eat, it's good."

I cautiously put it in my mouth and start to chew. It's salty and chewy, but also kind of sweet and refreshing. It's so strange that I don't even know how to describe it, but it tastes good. It feels like I'm eating something light and juicy, like fruit.

I finish chewing and say, "I like it!" Then I grab another one and pop it in my mouth.

Octo smiles. "Come, let's eat the rest of our food. It's hard to fill up on jellyfish."

Once we swim inside our ship, my first thought is that it's good to be home. I realize then that this place feels like home. I hadn't realized how much this had started to feel like my home until that moment.

I follow Octo to our nest, then we both settle in to eat.

As we're finishing up our food, Ovaggd'tho shows up. He greets us and then updates Octo on how the patrol went today.

"The beach was quiet. No humans around it. I think it will be a while before we have to worry about more humans on your beach."

Octo sighs, "I hope so, but Vrala seems uncertain."

Ovaggd'tho just nods and goes quiet for a few minutes. Finally, he looks between the two of us, and says, "Did everything go well with the healer?"

We both smile at him. Octo is the one that replies. "Yes, she's already pregnant. She'll have an egg like our people. We also went to the bones and received a blessing."

Ovaggd'tho gets a huge grin on his face then claps Octo on the back. "That's wonderful news! Xaiolpa will be so glad to hear it."

I laugh. I never expected to find an underwater bestie that would be excited about me being pregnant. "I can't wait to see what she says. Will you two be going to see Cindy off tomorrow?"

Ovaggd'tho scratches his mantle. "We're uncertain. We don't want to intrude."

"It wouldn't be intruding. I'm sure Cindy would be happy to see both of you."

Ovaggd'tho nods. "I'll tell Xaiolpa. We can meet you there."

We're all quiet for a minute, then Ovaggd'tho says, "I better go home now, Xaiolpa will be waiting for me...not patiently. She's excited to know what the healer said."

I laugh at that. I'm sure she'll attack him for info the moment he gets close to their home.

By the time he leaves, the ocean is beginning to get dark.

I use the bathroom, and when I come out, Octo is already settled into our nest.

I swim over and curl up next to him. As I'm lying there, thinking about the day and our future, Octo reaches over and runs his hand over my belly. Then he settles, resting it on my belly like he's protecting it.

I look up at him, and he quietly says, "Thank you, Naomi, for all you have given me. And thank you for giving me the chance to be a good mate to you."

I snuggle in closer to him, blinking back tears. "Thank you for finding me, Octo...although you definitely could have done that part better." I smile at him to let him know that I'm teasing.

He snorts and smiles at me. Then he begins stroking my belly.

I look down and say, "I wonder if it will be a boy or a girl." I suddenly think of all those videos I've seen of gender reveal parties where the dads get angry if it's a girl. I look up at Octo. "Does it matter to you if it's a boy or girl?"

He shakes his head. "I'll be happy with either. Either will be strong and fierce just like their parents."

I'm relieved and smile at that.

We quietly lay there for a few minutes, then I feel Octo's hand beginning to go lower as he strokes my belly.

He slides his hand down my stomach and then lower, brushing his finders through my pubic hair. Finally, he glides his knuckle through my pussy.

I whimper as he touches me.

He circles his knuckle around my clit, and I arch against him.

He replaces his hand with a tentacle and slides his hand up to cup my jaw as he kisses me. His tentacle slides through the folds of my pussy, then plunges into me, and I moan into his mouth.

He thrusts his tentacle into me, then two other tentacles slide up to join it.

I cry out as the three of them twine together on his next thrust. I'm stretched so full.

"Fuck...Octo." I manage to choke out.

Octo kisses me again, and as he's kissing me, I feel another tentacle slide up to my butt. He gently presses it into me. His kiss deepens and he continues pressing into me, further than he has before.

My nails claw at his chest, and I moan as he continues to slowly thrust his tentacles into my pussy and my ass. He's filling me completely.

I'm panting and can barely catch my breath, but I manage to say, "Octo, can I suck on one of your tentacles?"

His eye widens and he groans deep in his chest. A tentacle slides up to my mouth. I grab it and push the tip into my mouth, watching his face as I suck on it.

He gasps as he watches me. I pull it back out of my mouth and begin gently licking each sucker. His eye is locked onto me, watching every movement my tongue makes. I slowly circle my tongue around the surface of one final sucker, then I suck the tentacle back into my mouth and moan around it.

Octo rasps, "Naomi..."

He pulls the tentacles out of my pussy, and I whimper at their loss. I feel the tip of his cock slide through my pussy, and notch at my entrance. Then he swiftly presses into me.

I moan as he does. His tentacles feel amazing, but nothing is as thick as his cock. He pulls back and then thrusts into me harder this time.

I cry out, but it's muffled by his tentacle. I suck on it again and try to rub my tongue against the suckers as I do. Octo moans from the pleasure.

Then he begins thrusting the tentacle in my ass in time with each thrust of his cock.

I suck as much of his tentacle into my mouth as I can fit, and it muffles my squeals and moans. Octo thrusts into me and my entire body shudders in pleasure as he fills every empty place that I have completely full.

I cling to him as he fucks me. He's groaning loudly with each thrust. I feel another tentacle brush against my hip and then it teases my clit.

I nearly scream around his tentacle in my mouth, but Octo somehow manages to press more of it into my mouth. Then he latches a sucker onto my clit. I let out a muffled scream as the sucker flutters on my most sensitive spot. My whole body quakes as my orgasm crashes through me. I buck my hips and let out muffled cries as I come.

The waves of my orgasm begin to subside, but Octo's sucker is still clasped onto my clit. It's very quickly becoming overwhelming, I try to protest, but his tentacle is still in my mouth so all I can do is let out a whimper.

Octo lightly grazes his lips over my gills which causes me to shudder. Then he says, "We aren't done yet. I want you to come for me again."

I groan around his tentacle as the overwhelmed feeling melts away into pleasure. I feel another orgasm quickly building and my whole body begins to tremble. On his next thrust, I shatter. I moan and cry out around his tentacle as I come. I can feel my pussy squeezing his cock, and a moment later he yells as he comes.

He slowly pulls his tentacle out of my mouth then kisses me. As he's kissing me, he slowly begins sliding the tentacle out of my butt. I gasp and dig my nails into him as he does. Finally, he slides his cock out and I feel his seed spill out of me.

He hugs me to his chest and gently strokes his hand up and down my back. I feel several of his tentacles coil around me.

He kisses me again, twining his tongue with mine. After he's done kissing me, he strokes my hair and says, "Sleep, Naomi."

I lay my head against his chest and drift off immediately.

Chapter 35

I hold Naomi as she sleeps and slide my hand down to her belly to rest it there protectively.

I'm going to be a father. I keep repeating that in my head—I'm going to be a father.

I never dreamed that I would find a mate as perfect as Naomi. Then today we find out that she's already pregnant with my young. And when I took her to the whale graveyard, the bones blessed us.

Never before have I been this happy, not even when I earned my territory. It's like a dream.

I finally manage to drift off to sleep with my head full of thoughts of my perfect mate and the possibilities that lay ahead.

***

When morning comes, I expect to wake before Naomi. However, when I open my eye, she's still curled in my tentacles, already awake. And it looks like she's been crying.

I whisper, "Naomi, what is wrong? Why do you weep?"

She hiccups when she answers me. "Today I have to say goodbye to Cindy."

I don't know what to say to her. I know how much Cindy means to her. I run my hands through her hair. "I'm sorry, Naomi."

She just nods.

We lay like that for a while before she finally says, "I guess we should get up."

My hearts ache for her. This is my fault. "Naomi...I...I am sorry. This is because of me."

She shakes her head. "It's okay. It's not...I don't know...sometimes life just changes your relationships with people. This is one of those times. You kidnapping me pushed it along and sped things up, but like I said before, I think this would have happened anyway. We would have drifted apart."

She looks so sad. I run my palm down her back.

She takes a deep breath. "But...now I have you. I have this life, and a baby to look forward to. If you hadn't taken me, I would have still been saying goodbye to her as we all went home, but I would have been alone and lost. So, I'm glad it's happening this way."

I try to look at it from her point of view, but I still feel terrible. She must be able to see that on my face because she looks at me and whispers, "I don't blame you, so stop blaming yourself." Then she says, "I'm starving. Let's go find some food before we need to go to the beach."

We get up and swim out of the ship. I get my net out, and we go hunting for food.

As we catch crabs, I watch Naomi. She looks so natural in this environment. It doesn't look like she was recently living out of the water and walking around on land.

Once we fill the bag, we settle by a kelp forest to eat. Naomi watches a couple of seals playing in the kelp as she eats. Once she's full, she holds a leg of a crab out to one of the seals, wiggling it and enticing it to come to her. Seals don't take much convincing, and it swims right up to her, grabs the leg, and darts away into the kelp.

When we are done, we swim toward the reef.

As we near the reef, I see that Ovaggd'tho and Xaiolpa are already there. As soon as we swim up, Xaiolpa grabs Naomi in a big hug.

She has a huge smile on her face and her eyes are bright. "Ovaggd'tho told me that you're expecting young! And that the bones blessed you! I'm so excited for you! I cannot wait to help you with the...baby. Humans call it a baby, right?"

Naomi laughs, "Yes. Thank you. I'm excited too."

Xaiolpa turns to me and gives me a huge hug too.

Naomi looks anxious. "Have you looked to see if Cindy is here yet?"

They both shake their heads. Xaiolpa says, "We were waiting for you to get here."

Naomi smiles at Xaiolpa, then looks at me. I nod. "Let's go see."

The four of us swim up to the top of the reef. I go up to the surface and stick my head above water. I see Cindy and Nathan waiting on the beach. Nathan is standing in the sand, but Cindy has waded out into the water to about knee deep.

I do a quick scan of the beach to make sure no one else is there, and I'm pleased to see that it's just the two of them.

Both of them are scanning the horizon, looking for us. Nathan must see me because I notice him look in my direction and then get Cindy's attention.

I dip my head back into the water and sink down to Naomi. "They're waiting for you."

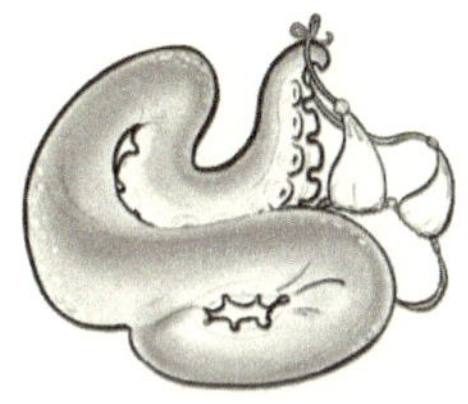

Chapter 36

Naomi

My heart leaps when Octo sinks back down and tells me that Cindy is waiting for me. I surge over the reef and swim straight toward the beach.

I can see a pair of feet and ankles under the water and I know it's her. I swim fast, and it takes no time for me to get to her. As soon as I'm close, I pop out of the water and say, "Cindy!"

Cindy leaps toward me and wraps me in a hug. It knocks both of us over into the water, and we both end up laughing. I look behind me and Octo, Xaiolpa, and Ovaggd'tho are all there watching. They're each above water until about their waists. Xaiolpa laughs and waves joyfully then says, "Hello, Cindy, Nathan!"

Octo and Ovaggd'tho are much more stoic when they say hello.

Cindy and Nathan both wave back.

I ask, "Are you two packed and ready to go?"

She laughs. "Yes...well except for a change in clothes." She shakes water off of her hands.

I cringe. "Yeah...you'll probably need to rinse off too. Sorry about that." I'm the one that has to be in the water, so I feel like it's my fault.

I watch her for a moment while she straightens out her wet clothes. I can't believe I'm not going to be able to see her except for when she travels here. The weight of this goodbye begins to press down on me. I can feel a knot forming in my throat and tears stinging behind my eyes.

Cindy looks up at me, then gives me a sad smile. She must have noticed the shift in my mood. She gives me another hug and says, "It's going to be okay, I promise."

I burst into tears then. I hug Cindy tightly and sob, "How?"

I hear her sniff. Her voice cracks when she says, "I don't know, but we'll make it work." Then she starts crying too and sinks down to her knees in the water, still holding onto me.

Octo swims over to us and begins to stroke my back.

I hear splashing as Nathan wades over to Cindy. He rests his hands on her shoulders to let her know he's there.

We are both still sobbing and clinging to each other.

Then Nathan clears his throat. "Um...well...I have a surprise for you two. I'd hoped to tell you before all the crying started."

Everyone turns to look at him.

"I hated seeing how upset Cindy has been. Before we knew that you were...um...alive, I called my father."

Cindy and I both look at him in shock. I'm sure Octo, Xaiolpa, and Ovaggd'tho are confused because they don't know Nathan the way we know him. But we know that Nathan hates his father. His father is extremely wealthy and extremely arrogant. He's the CEO of some tech company. When Nathan was little, his dad ran off with some hot younger woman, so Nathan has never had much of a relationship with him. During his teenage years, his father must have felt guilty, or more likely just wanted to appear to be a good father, so he started showing up and wanting a relationship with Nathan. But Nathan has never wanted anything to do with him.

Nathan continues, "I spoke with the owners of this resort. It's owned by an older couple. They have been very upset about Naomi's disappearance and supposed death. Along with all the police, detectives, and government agents, they also have true crime and unsolved mystery fanatics calling them all the time. Everyone wants to know what happened to Naomi, and everyone wants to come stay at the resort to look for clues. To make it even worse, the wife is extremely superstitious and is convinced Naomi's ghost is haunting the beach and resort. The wife firmly believes that Naomi's ghost stood over the bed while she was sleeping that first night after Naomi went missing. The couple wants nothing to do with any of it. They want to sell the resort. So, I called my dad and asked him for a favor—and well—he's agreed to give me the money to buy it. I've already made an offer to the couple, and they accepted it. I told them that Cindy wants to stay here to be close to Naomi's spirit. Anyway, we close on it tomorrow. I woke up early today and spoke with the couple and the attorney. It's all set and ready. We just have to sign everything and transfer the money. I was going to surprise both of you with it today."

We stare at him in shock.

Cindy finally speaks. "What? You mean...you mean that we will own this resort?"

Nathan nods. "Yep. We'll both have to quit our jobs or set up to work remotely, then we can run this place."

Cindy lets out a laugh. "What...oh my gods...*what*?"

I start laughing too.

Cindy then says, "But your dad?"

Nathan sighs then shrugs. "Yeah, the money came with strings attached. He wants to come visit twice a year and 'work to repair our relationship', whatever that means to him, but I can handle that. I just want you to be happy, Cindy, and there was no way you would ever be happy if you could only see Naomi once or twice a year."

Cindy lets go of me and flings herself into Nathan's arms. "Oh, my gods, thank you, Nathan." I hear her start crying onto his shoulder.

I'm still staring at him in shock. Octo leans over and says, "I don't understand. What happened?"

I look at him, and with tears in my eyes, I say, "This building and land..." I point to the resort and the beach. "Nathan owns it now. He bought it. They're not leaving. They're going to stay here. I'll be able to see Cindy every day." Then I start sobbing, and Octo wraps me in a hug.

Xaiolpa cheerfully says, "That's wonderful news." Then she looks at me. "And it will be so good once you have the baby too."

Cindy and Nathan go quiet and still, then Cindy turns to look at me. "A baby?"

I laugh nervously. "Um...surprise." I even do awkward jazz hands after I say it.

Cindy just stares at me. "You're pregnant?"

I nod then quickly explain, "We went to the underwater city to see the healer yesterday. We weren't sure if I could get pregnant. And if I did...well...if I would lay eggs or give live birth. So, we had to talk to the healer about it. She confirmed that I'm pregnant."

Nathan asks, "Underwater city?"

Cindy's eyes narrow. "What do you mean, lay eggs?"

I laugh nervously again. "Yeah, um...Octo's people lay eggs about halfway through the pregnancy. Then the eggs hatch later. The healer said that's what I'm going to do. Only it won't take as long as their pregnancies. And it's just one egg, not several."

Cindy's eyes get wide. "Oh." She just stares at me for a minute in shock. Then she says, "Okay." And she starts laughing. "Oh, my gods, you're pregnant!"

She flings herself back at me and gives me a huge hug. She rubs my belly and says, "I'm going to be the best aunt to this little baby." Then she continues to hug me as she says, "Oh! We'll have to get scuba equipment and learn to scuba dive. Then I'll even be able to babysit! Maybe we can set up a saltwater pool in the hotel so he or she can come stay the night."

I start laughing at the mental images that gives me. Then I break down into tears again while I'm still laughing.

Cindy laughs and wipes tears out of her eyes and then just hugs me.

We stay like that for several minutes, just holding each other. Both Nathan and Octo are patient and don't try to hurry us.

When we finally let go of each other, we are both wiping tears out of our eyes and laughing.

Cindy then looks at me and says, "Although if we're going to be hanging out, we should probably do something about a swimsuit for you. I can bring you something to wear when you come visit. Probably shouldn't have your boobs out all over the beach."

I look down and immediately begin blushing. I look up at her. "Oh my gods, I keep forgetting about that. I'm sorry, you guys." I cover my boobs with my hand and arm and then peek around Cindy and wave at Nathan. "Sorry, Nathan."

He just smiles. "Don't worry, I've just been trying to make sure I only look at your face."

Both Cindy and I start laughing again.

I finally say, "Oh my gods...I'm so overwhelmed. I was so upset and then I was so excited...and now I'm just exhausted."

Cindy gives me a concerned look. "It's been a lot of emotion today, but are you okay?"

Octo runs his hand over my hair. "It is probably the young you're growing. You have been very hungry the past couple of days."

Everyone is looking at me like I'm fragile, and that makes me feel uncomfortable. "Isn't it a bit early for me to be feeling anything because of the pregnancy? That shouldn't start for a few more weeks, right?"

Cindy shrugs. "Who knows; this isn't exactly a normal pregnancy for a human or one of Octo's people. If you're feeling tired, then you should probably just listen to your body. Why don't you go take a nap? I need to go change and unpack and get caught up on whatever is happening with buying this place. We can talk more later."

I smile. "Yeah, maybe a nap would be good."

Cindy and I give each other one last hug, and then Octo and I turn back toward the reef. Xaiolpa gives me a quick hug too, then she says, "You two go on, I have a couple of questions I want to ask Cindy about human baby customs."

I just smile at that. Xaiolpa is so sweet. I imagine she wants to find out if we have any ceremonies or customs for babies. Oh...that makes me wonder if they have any ceremonies or customs other than the blessing from the bones. I'll have to ask Octo about that.

Octo and I swim home, then he gathers some food for me. Once I've eaten, I curl up in his tentacles and fall asleep.

At some point, I wake up enough to realize that Xaiolpa and Ovaggd'tho have stopped by. I hear their hushed voices, and I think I hear them talking about humans, but I don't wake up enough to actually listen to what they're saying. I drift back to sleep to the soft sounds of them talking.

***

Later, Octo wakes me up and asks if I'm hungry. I stretch and still feel groggy, but my stomach growls at the thought of food, so I nod.

I sit up to uncurl myself from his tentacles expecting to need to swim and gather food, but he already has a net full of food waiting for us.

"Where did this come from? Did you leave while I was sleeping?"

He chuckles, "No, you were so wrapped up in my tentacles, I couldn't possibly have left without waking you up. Xaiolpa and Ovaggd'tho got these for us."

"Oh wow, that was so nice of them."

He hands me a crab, and I take a huge bite. We both end up eating our meal quietly. Once we're done, I sigh sleepily.

Octo is folding his net, and he stops and looks up at me. "Are you still tired, Naomi?"

I nod and rub my face. "Yes, I didn't sleep well last night because I was really upset about having to say goodbye to Cindy. Then all of the emotions today...plus...the baby..." I wave my hand in the direction of my stomach. "It wore me out."

He says, "We'll go back to sleep then. It's good for you to get your rest."

We curl back up in our nest, and I drift off to sleep almost immediately.

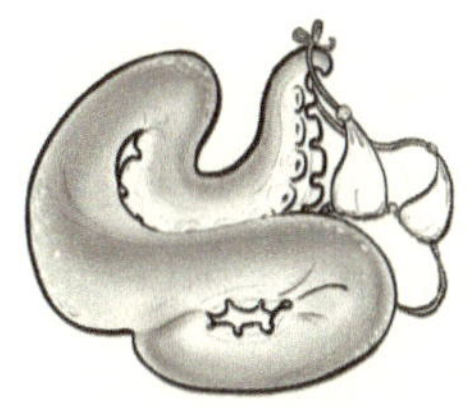

Chapter 37

I wake up the next morning and Octo is already awake. He's looking at me when I open my eyes, so I smile at him and say, "Hey."

He replies, "Good morning, my mate."

I rub my eyes and stretch as I start to wake up. "You seem to sleep less than I do."

He nods. "It does seem like you need a lot more sleep than I do. How long do humans usually sleep."

I yawn. "Hm. They recommend eight hours, but most people probably get less than that."

He gives me a curious look. "Who recommends it?"

I smile at that. Of course, he wouldn't know that phrase. "Doctors do."

He tilts his head at me, and I can tell he's confused.

I say, "Doctors are what we call healers."

"Ah." He furrows his brow. "Then why do humans not get that amount of sleep?"

That makes me chuckle. "I'm sure we should listen to them, but most people are just too busy. By the time they get everything done that they need to get done, there isn't enough time to do the things they enjoy."

He gives me a curious look. "What do they want to do, but don't have time for?"

I shrug. "Hobbies. Reading books maybe. Watching TV. Or making art. Or maybe they just want to look at their phone." None of these things are really things that can be done underwater, so I'm not sure if he's going to get it.

He watches me for a minute. "Are these things that you like to do?"

"Some of them. I like reading and watching movies. But...I can't really do those underwater." I'm not trying to make him feel bad, but there really isn't a way to say that without implying it's his fault.

He furrows his brow again and gets quiet for a few minutes. Finally, he says, "I don't like that you cannot do the things you enjoy."

I have no idea how to respond to this. I'm sure he's feeling guilty right now, and that's why he has that look on his face. I finally say, "Well, there's stuff I can't do up there that I can do down here."

He gives me a skeptical look. "Like what?"

I sigh dramatically, "I can't swim with amazing sea creatures. I can't float. I definitely can't run around naked all the time. And I don't have a tentacled mate up there."

He chuckles, and I wrap my arms around his neck and kiss him. Then I say, "If you're feeling guilty, don't. I'm happy here with you. And who knows, with Cindy here, maybe she really can build that saltwater pool in the resort. We could go there and...wait...can we stay out of water long enough to get up to the resort?"

He thinks for a minute. "I could. I assume you could, but I'm worried about trying it."

"Oh! Or we could have Cindy bring some sort of large white screen down to the beach and we could project a movie onto it so we could watch it from the water. And maybe I can have Cindy bring a book down to the beach. She could leave it in a small plastic storage container along with a small towel. Then I could take it somewhere private and sit in the water and read. The towel would be so I could dry my hands off before picking up the book, of course. See...no reason for you to feel guilty. If I want to do those things, we can find a way."

Octo gives me a doubtful look. I know probably none of that meant anything to him.

I just smile. "Just trust me. But really...even without those things, I'm happy here with you."

One of his tentacles slides up my back and over my shoulder, and he kisses me.

After he kisses me, I say, "But...I feel pretty guilty that you're just watching me sleep so much. Maybe I need to get used to the feeling of floating while I'm sleeping. We could braid some type of rope out of kelp and tie it around my ankle. Then we just tie the other end to something so I don't accidentally float away."

He raises his...well...where his eyebrows would be when I say that. Then he pointedly looks at the cage.

I gasp then point a scolding finger in his face. "No, not the cage. You better not even think about locking me in there, octopus."

He chuckles, then kisses me. "No, I learned that you don't like the cage. But don't worry about sleeping. It is not a hardship to hold my mate while she sleeps."

I'm not really convinced. Certainly, he's going to get bored sitting there holding me. But I can tell he's going to be stubborn about this for now, and there really isn't any point in trying to convince him. "Okay but promise me you will tell me if you get bored and we can figure out another way."

He scowls at me.

"I'm serious, Octo. I don't want you to resent me because you have to sit here bored all the time...so promise."

He studies my face for just a moment, and perhaps he can see just how stubborn I'm going to be about this too. Finally, he says, "Okay, I vow it."

I smile. "Good." I turn and glare at the cage, then I look back at Octo. "Why do you even have it? Was it on the ship already?"

"No, I found it and brought it here."

"You brought it here?! That must have been hard to move, Octo. Why did you bring it here?" I ask in disbelief.

He snorts, "It was not hard to move, not for a Guardian like me."

I roll my eyes at that.

He's quiet for a minute and then shrugs. "I thought it would be useful at some point. I thought maybe if I had young, they would like to play in it."

I raise my eyebrows. "Play in a cage? Please tell me you aren't planning on locking your children in there too."

He shakes his head. "No. It just seemed like something I would have enjoyed when I was young."

I think that's the first time he's brought up his childhood. I can't even imagine what his life would have been like. "What was it like when you were young?"

He's quiet for moment, then he sighs and says, "Lonely. I had lots of brothers and sisters, but I couldn't be close to any of them."

He glances at me, and I must have a confused look on my face because he continues, "My people, we're proud to protect our territories and our realm. We're proud to be strong fighters. Our territories are inherited from our father, but my people have lots of young. It means that the males must fight their brothers to win their territory. It ensures that the strongest son takes over protecting his father's territory. But it means that we are all enemies to each other from the moment we hatch."

"Oh, Octo, that sounds terrifying for a child." I hug myself close to him.

He nods. "It was. But it makes you strong...at least that's what my father always said."

This breaks my heart. Those poor kids. "So does that mean that you were alone all the time?"

"No. I had Ovaggd'tho. We've been friends for as long as I can remember. We helped train each other so that both of us would win against our brothers." He goes quiet for a minute, lost in thought. Then he smiles and says, "We also played a lot. When I found the cage, it made me think of playing when we were young. It's just the type of thing we would've spent all day playing in back then. I guess that's why I brought it here. I thought one day I would have a son that would want to do the same."

Oh my gods, I can feel tears starting to well up, and I sniff hoping to stop myself from crying.

Octo gives me a worried look. "Naomi, are you well?"

I sniff again, then start crying. "Y-yes. That was just so sad—but also sweet. I'm glad you had someone there for you when you were so alone." I take a deep, choked breath, then I continue, "In a way, our childhoods are very similar. We both were lonely and found a friend that was there for us no matter what."

He thinks about it for a minute, then smiles. "I guess we do have that in common."

I take a couple of deep breaths and shake off the sadness. I give him what is probably a pitiful look and say, "I'm sorry for the crying. It's probably the pregnancy."

Octo runs the back of his claw down my cheek. "Don't worry, Naomi. You have been through a lot."

We stay snuggled up against each other in our nest for a few minutes before we finally get up and start our day.

Something is bothering me now though. I started thinking about it after Octo told me his story. I can't let my kids fight each other; I won't let them fight each other like that. That's no way for kids to grow up. But this is Octo's culture. How do I tell him that?

I watch him as he folds his net. Finally, I decide that it's best to just say something now and get it over with. "Hey Octo, I don't want my children to be lonely like you and I were. I don't want them to grow up thinking of each other as enemies that have to fight each other to win this territory. We have to raise them a different way. I want them to feel loved by us and their brothers and sisters."

Octo watches me, thinking. It isn't long, but it feels like a lot longer. As each second drags on, I get more and more anxious about it. I'm telling him that I don't want to raise his children the way his people do. I don't know how he'll take that. My stomach starts feeling fluttery and I feel like I could cry again.

Finally, Octo nods and says, "Agreed. I don't want my young to feel like that either. We'll raise them better."

I let out a sigh of relief and swim into his arms. I wrap my arms around his neck and kiss him. "Thank you, Octo."

He holds me as I hug him. When I finally relax my grip on him, I smile at him. "So what are we doing today?"

"After we eat, we are going over to Xaiolpa's and Ovaggd'tho's cave so you can spend the day with Xaiolpa."

"That'll be fun. She's such a happy person. I enjoy spending time with her." I slide out of his grip so he can finish folding his net.

As soon as I start to swim to the other side of our nest, his tentacles wrap around me and drag me back against him. With my back against his chest, he wraps his arms around me and then kisses my shoulder. As his kisses work their way up my neck, I feel a tentacle slide between my legs and lightly graze over my pussy. I let out a small whimper from the faint touch.

Octo delves the tentacle deeper, parting the lips of my pussy. Then he teases me by slicking it through my folds, coating it with my wetness.

I moan and drop my head forward, watching his arms and tentacles wrap around me. He gently grabs my jaw and raises my head pressing it back against his shoulder. Then he wraps his huge hand around my throat, holding me in place.

I feel a tentacle wrapping around each of my thighs and pulling my legs apart. Spreading me for him. The tentacle teasing me dips into my heat the smallest amount. I gasp, then whimper as he pulls it away. He barely dips it into me again, teasing me more. I try to move my hips to press more of it into me, but Octo has me bound against his chest; I can hardly move. He pulls the tentacle out of me again.

I groan, then beg, "Octo...more please." His hand is still holding my throat, and I feel his teeth nip at my shoulder, then his tentacle presses into me a little bit more, but still not nearly enough.

I tremble against him. "Octo...please...I need more." I feel him flexing and moving behind me, then I feel something much thicker press against the entrance to my core. I gasp, suddenly realizing just how big his cock is. He's always used several tentacles to open me before he fucks me.

He slowly begins to press into me. I let out a loud cry when I feel myself begin to stretch around him. It's so intense and feels so good.

"Fuck...Octo...oh my gods." I gasp and moan as he presses into me. He continues to slowly press into me until he's buried deep inside me. We stay like that for just a minute while I adjust to the fullness.

Then he pulls nearly all the way out of me, and thrusts into me a little bit more quickly this time and I cry out loudly. As he thrusts into me again, he wraps one of his tentacles around my hips and snakes it down to the base of his cock so one of the suckers can latch onto my clit. I nearly scream when it does.

As his sucker works my clit, he begins thrusting into me harder and faster. My body trembles and I'm moaning and whimpering. When I'm at the very edge of my orgasm, he whispers in my ear, "Come for me, Naomi."

That pushes me over the edge. I cry out as I come. I try to writhe in his grip, but he's still holding me in place. I feel my pussy squeeze around his cock as he continues to thrust into me.

On his next thrust, he buries his cock inside me and growls as he comes, filling me with his seed. We are both breathless and panting once he's done.

He loosens his grip on me, and I practically float away from him as limp as a noodle.

He laughs and turns me around as he pulls me back toward him. Then he kisses me. His tongue brushes against my lips and I open for him. It delves into my mouth, claiming me.

When we finally pull apart, I whisper, "Octo...fuck...that was good."

He just smiles at that. "Sometimes my mate does want to be told what to do."

I huff at that and roll my eyes.

He holds me for a while before he finally says, "We should get you to Xaiolpa."

Chapter 38

Naomi and I swim to meet Xaiolpa at her place. Naomi grabs a few crabs to eat along the way, and I catch several fish for myself.

Once we get there, I kiss Naomi goodbye and tell her I'll be back in a little while, then I swim off.

Once I'm out of sight, I check my pouch to make sure I still have the pearl safely tucked away. I let out a sigh of relief when I feel it. I've been so afraid of losing it. Of course I could always find another pearl, but I want it to be this pearl from our first meal together.

I swim out of my territory and head in the direction of Cthegril. I swim hard and fast. The metalsmiths are just outside of Cthegril on the shore, and I don't want to be gone so long that Naomi becomes suspicious.

After what feels like ages of swimming, I'm relieved when I see the faint outline of the buildings in the distance.

I swim towards the shore on the northern side of the city. There are docks and warehouses here where land Guardians and Elven work and trade with those of us that live in the water.

The Merfolk work with land dwellers all the time. They depend on them for their buildings and much of the stuff in their homes. My people typically only deal with them for metal weapons or jewelry.

I swim up to the dock. There's a ramp that enters into the water to make it easier for us to come out of the water, but there's also a ladder off one side of the dock. Typically, only the Elven use the ladder, but there's a large merman already on the ramp, and using the ladder is not a hardship for me. I grab the bottom rung and begin pulling myself up using my arms. I pull myself all the way up, then use my tentacles to pull myself over onto the dock.

When I land on the dock, one of the Elven notices me. "Guardian, are you here to see one of the smiths?"

I nod. "It's for jewelry."

He nods and yells something into the back of the warehouse. A couple of minutes later, a strong-looking, purple Elven wearing a leather apron comes out of the warehouse and walks up to me.

He's tall, but out of the water and raised up on my tentacles, I'm much taller than he is. He barely comes up to my chest.

He looks up at me and says, "Hello. You're looking for jewelry?"

"Yes." I pull the pearl out of my pouch and hand it to him. "I would like this made into a necklace for my mate."

He looks at the pearl, then says, "That will be easy enough. Do you want gold or silver? Any extra stones added to it?"

I reply, "No other stones, just this pearl." Then I look at him thoughtfully before asking, "Do you know the rings that humans exchange when they have a wedding? What metal are they made of?"

He looks at me curiously. "I know of them, they're usually made of gold."

I nod. "Then make it from gold."

He gives me an assessing look. Then he says, "Why human? Is your mate a human?"

His question makes me wary, but I answer. "She was a human. My mating bite changed her so she can live underwater with me. I want to give her something that will honor her human customs." I look down and flex my hand. "And we cannot wear rings."

"I see. It's no problem; I can make it a necklace. I'm sure it will mean the same to her." He gets out some parchment and begins making notes for the order. As he's writing, he says, "Your mate isn't the only human mate I've heard about recently. There was a big mess with one of the lords not too long ago. He stole a Guardian's human mate and tried to keep her for himself. It didn't end well for him. He was a terrible Elven anyway—got what he deserved. Out of his mind to even think to steal a Guardian's mate." The Elven is shaking his head as he talks and writes.

When he's done writing, he looks up at me and chuckles. "Sorry, I'm a talker. I'm sure none of what the lords up here do matters much to you guys out there in the deep."

I shake my head.

We work out the details, then he gives me the total. I give him half the coin now and the other half will be due when it's ready tomorrow. I'll have to get Naomi to stay with Xáiolpa again then. Hopefully Ovaggd'tho won't mind covering my territory once again.

I thank him when we are done, then dive off the dock into the water.

I swim home as quickly as I can.

Once I get back to my territory, I swim off to find Ovaggd'tho.

He's swimming along one of the borders when I find him. I explain that the necklace will be ready tomorrow.

He gives me a big grin. "Xaiolpa will enjoy spending the day with Naomi again. She loves Naomi and is so excited to have a friend nearby." He pauses for a minute, then shakes his head. "You may have started something though; she's started talking about young. We may have to pay a visit to the healer soon."

I give him a big grin. I like the thought of both of us having young soon.

He pats me on the shoulder. "Don't worry about tomorrow. I'll watch your territory and Xaiolpa will be happy to spend time with Naomi."

I clasp his hand in gratitude, then spontaneously wrap my other arm around him to hug him. "Thank you for all that you've done to help us."

He seems startled for a moment, then he hugs me back.

After we release each other, I say, "Now I must go to the beach and see if I can catch Cindy or Nathan to talk about the surprise."

We say goodbye to each other and swim off in different directions.

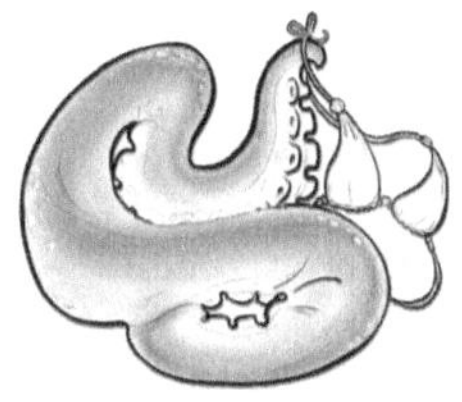

Chapter 39

Naomi

I enjoy my day with Xaiolpa. We swim around gathering more kelp, then spend the day working on more netting. She spends most of the time talking excitedly about the baby. I'm pretty sure she has baby fever. And I'm a terrible friend, because I'm so distracted that I don't pay much attention to all the things she's saying. I keep getting lost in thought. I try to imagine what it's going to be like having a little tentacled baby, and raising them under water, but I just have so much trouble envisioning it.

It's at least a few hours before Octo shows back up.

When he swims back up, he gives me a large sharp toothed grin. I'm relieved to see him because I was starting to get tired, and I'm ready to go home and rest.

Octo must notice that something is off with me because his face drops into a look of concern and he immediately swims to me and brushes his knuckles against my cheek.

"Are you okay, Naomi?" He's so sweet when he asks, and my heart swells at his concern.

Xaiolpa sets down the net she's working on and swims to my side with a look of concern on her face too.

I nod. "Yeah, I'm just tired." I rub a hand over my eyes. "I think the baby is making me tired."

Octo scoops me up in his arms and says, "I'll carry you home then."

We say our goodbyes, and Octo swims off with me in his arms. I lean my head against his chest and doze on the short swim back to our home.

When we get close, Octo gently wakes me and says, "Are you hungry, Naomi?"

I nod. He gently sets me down in the sand on the ocean floor and gets out his net. We spend a few minutes swimming around, gathering crabs and oysters for me, and fish for Octo. Then we swim into the ship and to our nest.

I don't end up eating very much, I eat just enough so that I'm not starving. Once I'm done, I curl up in his tentacles and fall fast asleep.

***

I sleep straight through the night, and before I know it, Octo is gently waking me up. I try to nuzzle back into his tentacles, and I hear him chuckle.

He runs his hand down my back and says, "Naomi, it is time to wake up."

I groan and grumble, then press my face more tightly against him.

He chuckles again, still stroking my back.

I let out a muffled sigh. "Let's just stay in bed today."

I hear concern in his voice when he says, "Are you still tired?"

I feel bad that he's worried. I'm fine, I just want to be lazy and snuggle. So, I nod and then stretch. "Yes, but don't worry, nothing's wrong. I just like snuggling and sleeping with you."

I look at him, and he has a big grin on his face as he watches me. He leans down and kisses me, then says, "Xaiolpa is going to come here today while I patrol my territory."

"What? How do you know that? I didn't hear her say that when we were leaving yesterday."

He smiles. "She stopped by while you were sleeping yesterday. She was worried about how tired you were, so she came by to check on you. Then she offered to come here and stay with you while I'm out today."

It still bothers me that he seems to want me to have a babysitter while he's gone, but then again, I don't really want to be bored and alone either. I think it over for a few minutes, then I say, "I appreciate you getting her to stay with me...but...you know I can also stay by myself at some point too...right?"

He looks down and I think I catch a small grimace on his face. "I know. I just...I still worry."

I push up to his face and say, "I'm not going anywhere." Then I kiss him.

His tentacles wrap around me, pulling me closer to him as he deepens our kiss.

Just then, there's a little knock on the 'door' to our nest. I pull away from Octo and turn to see Xaiolpa floating at the entrance. She giggles when I look at her.

I smile at her as Octo loosens his tentacles' grip on me and lets me go.

She swims over to us and studies me. "Did you sleep well, Naomi? Are you more rested, or do you need to sleep more while Octhogh'xu is out?"

"I'm fine. I slept well, and I feel a lot better today."

She smiles. "Good! Today we are going to work on a sling for you to carry the baby in. It's similar to making a net, we just knot the kelp more closely together."

This gets me excited. "Perfect! I was wondering what kind of things I would need for the baby. Human babies need a lot of stuff."

Both Octo and Xaiolpa give me a curious look. Xaiolpa says, "They do?"

I nod. "Yes, tons of stuff. We have special parties for pregnant moms so they can get a lot of what they need as presents."

Xaiolpa says, "What kind of things do they need? They're just babies; how can they need a lot?"

I suddenly realize that living underwater probably means that you don't need nearly as much stuff. It's not like I'll need a car seat, or clothes, or even diapers. "Oh—well—you need a baby bed, a changing table, a lot of clothes, tons of diapers, bottles, one of those little baby bathtubs...." I stop listing things when I see the looks on both of their faces. They're both furrowing their brows in confusion. They clearly have no idea what I'm talking about and can't even imagine needing that stuff.

Xaiolpa asks, "Human babies need all of that?"

I self-consciously nod.

She continues, "Well...don't worry. You won't need nearly that much for a Guardian baby."

I smile awkwardly at that.

"We'll make a sling today. It would probably be good to have more than one. We can make one to fit Octhogh'xu too."

With that, Octo kisses me and says, "I'm going to patrol for a while. Be sure to eat something."

I smile about him fussing over me. "Don't worry, I'm starving; I'll definitely eat."

Xaiolpa looks at me. "Oh! Then we better catch some food. We must feed that baby."

We swim toward the ocean floor as Octo swims off to patrol his territory.

Chapter 40

I swim as quickly as I can back to the metalsmith's dock. When I get there, I meet with the same talkative Elven smith that I spoke with yesterday.

He brings a small fabric pouch out to me. He pulls the necklace from it, and hands it to me. The pearl is enclosed in a small golden cage and hangs from a golden chain. It shimmers and sparkles as the light hits it. It's more beautiful than I ever imagined it could be. Now I understand why humans are drawn to these small pearls.

"It's very beautiful. I think she'll like it very much. Thank you, smith."

He smiles and says, "Glad you're pleased with it."

I pay him the remaining coin that I owe. Then I carefully put the necklace back into the little fabric pouch and tuck it safely into my pouch with my net.

I give my thanks to the smith again. Then I dive off the dock and into the water and begin my swim home.

***

I make good time on my swim back.

As soon as I'm back in my territory, I hunt down Ovaggd'tho. When I find him, he greets me happily. "How is Naomi today? Xaiolpa was very worried about how tired she was yesterday."

"She's well. She told me not to worry."

He smiles. "Good. I know Xaiolpa will fuss over her and take care of her." He pauses. "Were you able to get the necklace?"

I nod and take it out to show him. I explain what Naomi told me about humans valuing pearls.

He laughs and shakes his head. "Humans value them—and to think, we just throw them away!" He pauses to look at the necklace again. "I'm sure she'll be very pleased with it."

"I hope so." I tuck it back safely into my pouch. "I'm going to the beach to finish up last minute plans for tomorrow."

Ovaggd'tho nods. "See you tomorrow."

I smile as I swim away.

***

I quickly make my way to the beach.

As I get close to the reef, I see that Vrala is already there. He greets me as I swim up.

"Hello, Octhogh'xu. I heard that you wanted to see me."

"Yes, I wanted to ask a favor of you..." I quickly explain the surprise we have planned for Naomi tomorrow.

He smiles and agrees to it. "I think that'll be a wonderful surprise for her. I'm also glad you wanted to see me. I need to talk to you about the humans."

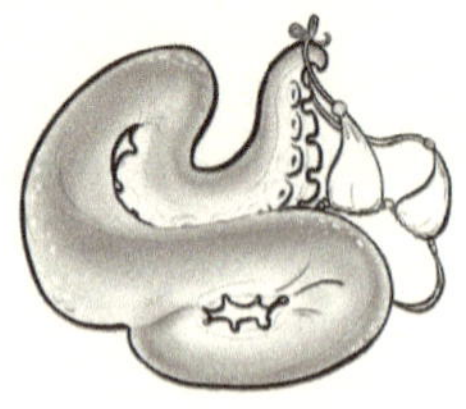

Chapter 41

Naomi

Xaiolpa and I spend the day laughing and talking while we gather kelp and she shows me how to make a sling to hold the baby.

Xaiolpa definitely has baby fever, she spent most of the time talking about babies. I wouldn't be surprised if she ends up going on a trip to the healer to undo whatever magical birth control they have in place.

I think about it as I work on the sling, and I kind of like the idea of us being pregnant at the same time. I always secretly hoped that Cindy and I could have babies near each other so we could be pregnant together and experience it all together. But you can't really pick when you're going to find the right person to have a baby with.

Once Cindy got engaged, I kind of let go of that idea. She was already about to be married, and I didn't even have a decent boyfriend that I was seeing—scratch that—I didn't even have a decent guy that I could even start seeing.

I think about how I was a bit depressed about it for a few days after I found out about Cindy's engagement. I never let her know, of course, but I definitely had to take time to let go of that dream.

My fingers pause while tying the knot that I'm working on when it suddenly hits me that it did actually work out. Now I have Octo, and I'm pregnant. Cindy just got married. We could absolutely end up pregnant at the same time.

And now I also have Xaiolpa. She's completely different than Cindy. She's sweet in comparison to Cindy's feistiness, but she's turning into another best friend. She was right there with me when Octo was taken. And she's been right here with me, helping me, this whole time. From the moment she discovered that Octo had me locked in a cage, she's been there for me.

I look up at her and smile and a little bubble of happiness floats up inside me.

She gives me a curious look. "Naomi, are you feeling well?"

I feel tears forming behind my eyes. I sniff and then nod. "Yes, I was just thinking."

She tilts her head curiously. "About what?"

"I was just thinking about how grateful I am to have you as a friend." Then I suddenly fling myself at her and wrap her in a hug. I start sniffling and crying as soon as I hug her.

She hugs me back and pets my hair. "I'm happy to have you as a friend too. I think the baby may be making you emotional today, Naomi."

I sniff as we let go of each other. My voice is choked when I say, "Probably so. But I really am glad to have you as a friend."

She pats my hand. "And I'm glad too."

***

When Octo comes home a little while later, Xaiolpa and I are inside the ship. I excitedly show him the sling I've been working on. It's nearly finished, and I'm so proud of it.

He smiles when he sees it, then runs his fingers over the knots.

"It's very nice, Naomi."

Xaiolpa has a huge grin on her face as she watches me. "She's so good at it; she's a fast learner."

I smile at that, then hold the sling up in front of me and say, "I should be able to finish it up tomorrow."

I wrap it around my body and try to imagine a little baby tucked inside.

A thought occurs to me... "Octo, will our baby have tentacles like you or legs—well, flippers, I guess—like me?"

He pauses for a minute. "Probably tentacles since your body was made to go with mine." Then he swims over to me and scoops me up into his tentacles. I startle and squeal as I fall back into them. They catch me, holding me weightless.

Xaiolpa smirks and says, "I'll leave you two alone now. I'll see you later."

I wave goodbye just as Octo leans down and kisses my shoulder, then grazes his mouth up my neck and over my gills. I shiver from the soft touch of his mouth against my gills.

His tentacles twist around my body, binding me as he kisses his way up to my mouth. I feel a tentacle slide through my heat, and I whimper softly against his lips.

He presses his body against mine as he kisses me, and I wrap my legs around him. While we kiss, his tentacles begin shifting us so that he ends up on his back. His tentacles twist more tightly around my body, pinning me against his hips. I'm pinned so tightly against him that the webbing between the base of his tentacles encloses around my hips and waist.

His cock has already extruded, and I press my pussy against it. We both groan at the sensation.

Trapped in his coils, I can barely move, but I'm able to move just enough to grind against his cock. So, I begin to slowly move my hips. It puts just the right amount of pressure on all the right spots, and soon I begin moaning.

Octo watches me, his one good eye wide. He gasps occasionally as I pick up my pace.

As I grind against him, I begin to feel an orgasm building. But just before it peaks and I fall over that edge, it slips away, and I groan in frustration.

"Octo, please...I need more." This causes him to groan so deep that he practically growls. I feel it vibrate through his chest. "Please, Octo, I need you inside me."

His tentacles loosen their grip on me just slightly and I feel two of them slip underneath me. They latch around my thighs and raise me up. I feel his cock press against the entrance to my core. Then he drags me down onto his cock, and I moan as he slides into me.

His tentacle webbing is still enclosing me, and I still can't move, so he uses the tentacles wrapped around my thighs to lift me and fuck me. Each thrust getting harder than the last until I'm gasping as his cock slams into me.

I'm pressed so tightly against him that my clit grinds against the suckers around his cock pocket, and I gasp loudly. "Fuck, Octo…"

Octo plunges his cock back into me, burying himself deep inside and grinding me against him again. An orgasm suddenly explodes through me. Octo's limbs still have me enclosed and hold me tightly in place, but my muscles quake and spasm as the pleasure rolls through me. Octo's breath shudders and then he groans as he comes.

We are both panting by the end of it.

Octo unfurls his tentacles from around me, and I sink down next to him and fall asleep.

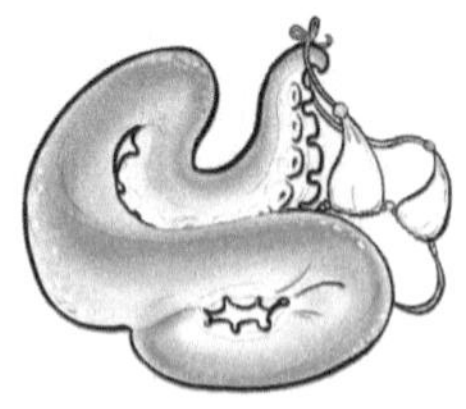

Chapter 42

I sleep through the night, all the way to morning. I wake up to the sound of Octo gently whispering, "Naomi..."

I groan and bury my face against his side.

"Naomi, we need to get up."

I groan again, then whimper. "Sleep..."

I feel the rumble in his chest as he chuckles. "Come, we need to get up." He pauses for a minute like he wants to say more, then he says, "I have a surprise."

I lazily lift my head and look at him. Then I groggily mumble, "Really? What kind of surprise?"

He chuckles again. "You'll have to get up to find out."

That wakes me up a little. "You really have a surprise for me?"

He just gives me a knowing grin, taunting me.

I stretch and get up. "Okay, I'm up. What's the surprise?"

Octo shakes his head. "So impatient. Follow me." I follow him as he swims out of our nest and out of the sunken ship.

Octo pauses as soon as we're outside and gets out his net. "Come, let's catch breakfast, then I'll take you to your surprise."

I huff in pretend irritation. "You're really going to make me wait to tell me what the surprise is."

He grins and nods in response.

I narrow my eyes at him, then mumble, "Fucking octopus."

He just chuckles at me as he starts to swim off. We harvest some oysters and catch several crabs. Octo catches a large eel along with a few fish. Once we have enough, we stop to eat. We eat quietly without talking, but I spend my time watching him suspiciously, trying to figure out what he's up to.

Once we're done, Octo folds up his net, then he takes my hand. "Come." He pulls me in the direction of the beach. I swim alongside him, still trying to figure out what he's planning.

When we get to the reef, Octo swims up to the top and peers over.

I follow him, and peer over the reef just after he does. What I see near the beach surprises me. I see Xaiolpa, Ovaggd'tho, and the other Sea Guardian, Vrala. I also see a couple of pairs of human legs in the water to about knee deep.

I pop my head above water and see Cindy and Nathan standing in the water. When Cindy sees my head, she waves.

What are they all up to?

I duck my head back underwater and look at Octo. He's smiling hugely at me.

I finally say, "What's going on?"

He just smiles at me. "Come, let's go." He takes my hand and pulls me over the reef and toward the beach.

When we get near, Xaiolpa, Ovaggd'tho, and Vrala join us, and we swim up to where Cindy and Nathan are. We all push our upper bodies out of the water when we get there.

The first thing I see once my face is out of the water is Cindy grinning at me.

I look around at everyone bewildered, "You guys are up to something."

She just grins at me. "Octo can tell you."

He comes up to stand just next to me and takes my hand. When I look at him, he says, "I know that our mating wasn't...traditional for you..."

I raise my eyebrows at that, but don't interrupt him.

He continues, "So I wanted to give you...a wedding. I thought—hoped—that you would be pleased to have a human mating ceremony."

I'm completely shocked. "A wedding? You want to have a wedding like humans?"

Cindy speaks up then. "He arranged for Vrala to be the wedding officiant, and for the rest of us to be here."

My eyes immediately fill with tears and I look back at Octo. "Thank you, Octo...this is...this means so much." I wrap my arms around his neck and kiss him. I can feel tears rolling down my cheeks as we kiss.

After a minute of us kissing, Vrala clears his throat. We stop and turn to look at him.

Cindy hands Vrala a piece of paper and says, "Here's what you should say." She talks to him for just a moment, pointing at different parts of the paper.

Once she's explained it all to him, she walks over to stand off to my side. I realize then that Ovaggd'tho and Xaiolpa are standing together off to Octo's side.

Vrala gets into place in front of us, then begins to speak. "We have gathered here today in honor of Naomi's human heritage to celebrate the joining of two souls in a lifelong commitment of love and devotion. Naomi and Octhogh'xu—"

Octo interjects, "Octo."

Vrala stops speaking and gives him a confused look.

Oct says, "I would like to go by Octo. That's the name that my mate calls me."

I beam a huge smile up at Octo as he says that.

Vrala nods and then continues, "Naomi and Octo have certainly already withstood trials and proven their love to each other. We all wish them the best of happiness and the smoothest of waters in the future." Vrala then nods to Octo.

Octo turns to me and begins opening the pouch he keeps his net in. He pulls out a tiny package and begins to open it. He says, "I know the human tradition is rings, but we can't wear them. I hope this will suffice." He pulls a gold necklace out of the package and then reaches around my neck to put it on me. I look down with wide eyes. The pendant is a small golden cage with a pearl inside. I recognize the pearl immediately. It's the one he threw on the ground during our first meal together—when I was so shocked by his actions.

Once he's done putting it on me, he takes my hands and says, "I vow to stay by your side, protect you, care for you, and love you for all the days of my life."

My eyes fill with tears again and I choke back a sob. "Oh, Octo—I vow to stay by your side, protect you, care for you, and love you for all the days of my life too."

I fling myself into his arms and press my mouth against his in a passionate kiss. We each try to devour the other, and Vrala has to clear his throat again to interrupt us.

We stop and turn back toward him.

He looks at the paper and says, "By the authority vested in me, I now pronounce you husband and wife. You may now kiss...again."

Cindy and Xaiolpa both giggle.

I laugh and kiss Octo again, but this time I try not to get too lost in it.

We kiss until we hear everyone clapping. When we break our kiss, Octo says, "I hope you liked this. I wanted to give you what you could have had in your world."

With tears streaming down my cheeks I say, "It's perfect. You've given me everything I could have dreamed of and so much more."

Then I kiss him again.

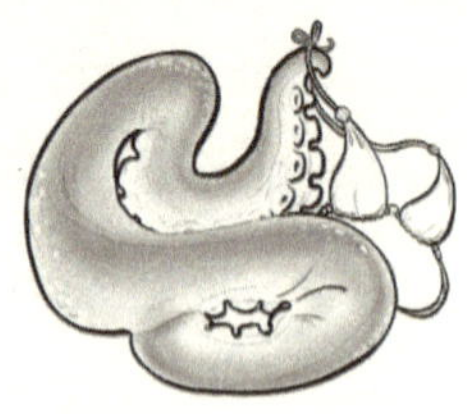

Chapter 43

Naomi

Two weeks later

A couple of weeks after our wedding ceremony, there's a knock on the side of the hull of our ship early one morning. A male voice sharply calls, "Octhogh'xu." Octo and I both wake up immediately.

Octo looks bewildered. "It's Vrala."

We both swim outside, and Vrala is there waiting for us. He's in that form that looks beautiful and crystalline.

He nods to both of us and says, "I'm sorry to wake you and your mate, but your help is needed."

Octo's hand drifts to his pendant, the one that his people use to call for help. Vrala notices it too and shakes his head. "We don't need to call for all the Guardians for a fight. We need your mate's opinion on something."

Octo turns a wide eye to me, and I say, "Me...what do you need my opinion on?"

Vrala gives us a grim look. "The humans are back."

I gasp and cover my mouth. Octo tenses and immediately begins asking questions. "Where? I don't feel humans on my territory. Are we needed for battle?"

My stomach flips with fear, and I place my hand over my belly. Octo can't go back into battle. The last time was terrible. I can't do that again...and now I'm pregnant. My chest starts to feel tight and I feel tears burning behind my eyes.

Vrala puts out his hands in a calming manner. "No no...we don't need to go to battle yet. We've been watching the facility that we freed Octhogh'xu from, and humans have shown up to survey the damage and to clean up. We expected that, and we've kept an eye on it, hoping that they would just go away once they were done. Now more humans are showing up. They're bringing large machines with them and supplies. We think they're going to rebuild. We want to get your opinion on what they're doing."

I close my eyes in dread and nod. "They probably are coming back. Everything was so overwhelming for me...freeing Octo...the pregnancy...it was naïve of me to think they would just be gone. That's not how humans work. They want to discover and explore and...conquer, if they can. I should've realized that and warned you."

Vrala gives me an understanding look. "You didn't fail us. We knew that we needed to keep an eye on them and were already doing it. The Guardians with territory nearest to the wreckage have been watching it and reporting back to me."

I nod and give Octo a defeated look. "So, what do I need to do? Just come look?"

Vrala nods. "We just want you to explain to us what you see happening. Your territory is far enough away that we wouldn't need help from Octhogh'xu to battle them. If the threat is big enough, we will bring in soldiers to protect it."

My eyes go wide. "You have soldiers?! I thought it was just Guardians protecting territories. I didn't know you had an army!"

Vrala smiles. "Of course we have soldiers. If humans did invade us, we would need more than just the handful of Guardians living here to fight them."

I'm truly shocked. What he says makes perfect sense, but I never even considered that they would have a military of any kind.

Vrala says, "Come, we should go now. There are others waiting there for us."

That catches me off guard. "There are?"

Vrala just nods.

Octo gets his spear and we follow Vrala to the facility.

The swim to the facility seems to take a lot longer than it did the day Octo was taken. Memories from that day flood my mind as we travel there. I remember the fear and horror I felt when they captured him. Then realizing that they were going to transport him over land to another location...I felt so hopeless. And, oh gods, when they tried to drown Cindy and Nathan...

I feel my heart start racing and I realize that I need to get my thoughts under control. Octo notices and reaches his hand out to mine. He squeezes my hand then quietly says, "Naomi, are you well?"

I nod. "Yes, just memories...from that day."

He squeezes my hand to reassure me then says, "I understand. I have them too."

We spend the rest of the trip there swimming in silence. Eventually I begin to see the shadow of the underground structure in the distance beyond the reef.

As we get closer, I notice people waiting for us at the reef. There are two Guardians that look like Octo, another Sea Guardian that looks like Vrala, and a merman with bright red and orange coloring. Then there's a massive one that I've never seen before.

We swim up to the group and all eyes turn to me. Each of them looks surprised to see someone like me, and I realize that most probably haven't seen a human that's been mated to a Guardian. It intimidates me a little bit to be the focus of so many males. Before their scrutiny becomes too uncomfortable, Octo introduces me by saying, "This is my mate, Naomi."

I can't do anything but stare at the massive new type of Guardian. He must be one of the soldiers that Vrala mentioned. He's huge. Octo and the merman are big, but this Guardian is even bigger than them. He has four arms and two legs. He's standing stoically on the ocean floor with his top set of arms crossed over his chest, his left lower hand is on his hip, and right lower hand holds a massive spear like Octo's—only bigger.

He's covered in hard, spiked plate armor that looks like it's similar to a spiky crab shell. Even his head is plated and almost looks like he's wearing a helmet. The plates are a mottled brown color that's clearly camouflage for blending in with the sand. His hands are clawed much like Octo's. His feet are bare and also have long claws. His skin is milky white, and he has huge eyes that are an unearthly, solid black. He doesn't have a nose; instead, he just has nostril slits where a nose would be. His teeth are sharp like Octo's, but his mouth is framed on either side by some sort of stiff, bristled appendage that reminds me of the mandibles on an insect.

Vrala quickly introduces all of the males present, but I'm so overwhelmed that I barely catch anyone's name. I'm aware enough to pick up on the fact that these are all very important people. These are leaders of some sort. I smile nervously at each of them. I'm studying them when I hear Vrala say, "Naomi was human, she's going to observe the humans and tell us what she thinks they're doing, and if it's dangerous to our world in her opinion."

I look at Vrala then and realize the gravity of what I'm doing here. Anxiety spirals inside me. It looks to me like my opinion will decide if they prepare for a battle of some kind. I don't want that kind of responsibility. What if I get the answer wrong? What if I think it's safe and then humans attack and they aren't prepared?

Octo distracts me by putting his hand on my back and saying, "Come, Naomi, let's go look." Then we swim away from the others and to the top of the reef. I turn to Octo and frantically say, "Octo, what if I'm wrong? What if I tell them it's safe and it's not?" My heart is pounding.

"Shhh, Naomi, they only want your opinion on what the humans are doing. They will make their decisions based on more than that. Don't worry."

I nod.

He strokes my cheek and says, "Just look and tell them what you see. That's all you have to do."

I nod again and look up at the glow of the sun breaking through the water. Octo takes my hand and we both swim up to the surface to look above.

When my head first breaks the surface, I feel the now familiar sharp sting of my delicate skin being exposed to air. It takes my eyes a few moments to adjust to the brightness of the sun, but once they do, I'm able to look around me.

When I look at what remains of the facility, I'm confronted with a flurry of activity and sounds. I hear the echoing sounds of construction and see that they've torn most of the wreckage down. It looks like they are leveling it. I sigh as I see pallets of building supplies being unloaded from freight trucks. They're definitely planning to rebuild.

There are a lot of vehicles parked around the construction site, and several of them look suspiciously like military or government vehicles.

As I look at the workers, I notice a few people in military uniforms inspecting the area. There's a woman in uniform that's flanked by several other people in military uniforms. I can't see the details of her uniform from here, but she commands the attention of all the others as if she's their leader. She definitely looks important; she must be some sort of general. She glares out toward the ocean, scrutinizing it. Fortunately, she hasn't looked in our direction yet. Shit...this is bad.

Octo and I duck our heads back under water to avoid being seen. I give him a dark look, then we swim back to the group.

All of them look at me expectantly, but I see that none of them have hope in their eyes. I take a deep breath and say, "It looks like they're rebuilding." The group lets out a collective breath of disappointment and nod. This is exactly what they were expecting. I add, "It's worse than that though. I saw some people in military uniforms. They looked like officers and maybe a general."

The merman says, "Not surprising. We've known something like this was coming for a long time. The divide between our two worlds is getting weaker, and it's getting harder to protect the places where our worlds touch. More and more humans have ended up accidentally—or purposefully—in our world. And there are rumors of some of our people ending up in their world. All of this draws the attention of the humans."

My mind catches on where he says that more and more humans have ended up here. There are others like me? I look at Octo, but he's listening to what they're saying.

The merman continues, "I will meet with the Elven and one of the Mountain Guardians about what can be done along this border."

They all nod and then are quiet for a minute. Finally, the armored Guardian speaks. His voice is deeper and more gravely than any voice I've ever heard. "I'll begin preparing soldiers."

Vrala says, "We'll all begin our preparations." He then looks at me, "Thank you, Naomi, for your insight." He nods to Octo next, and it feels like a dismissal.

Octo looks toward all of these...leaders and nods. Then he takes my hand and begins to pull me toward home. I quickly nod to them too.

We swim home in silence. Once we get there, I give Octo a worried look. "Octo, I'm afraid."

He gently cups my cheeks in his hands. "You don't need to be afraid. We're safe. They'll send soldiers to act as extra Guardians in the territories closest to where humans are building."

"But what about your territory?"

Octo smiles. "Do you really think Cindy would let those humans come down to the beach to try to attack us again?"

I smile at that. "No, she wouldn't."

"If they become a problem near us, Vrala will do the same here. He'll send soldiers to help defend my territory. Don't worry about it anymore, my mate. If the humans were to attack my border again, we would handle it together with Ovaggd'tho, Xaiolpa, Cindy, and Nathan at our sides." Then he kisses me.

***

My fears subside and over the next couple weeks, I try to forget my worries about the facility and humans. I just enjoy my new mate and my new life. Octo is right; no matter what comes along, we can handle it together.

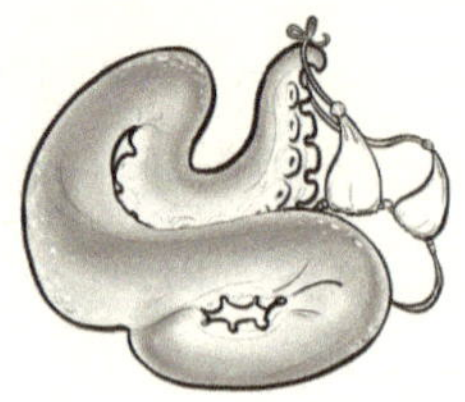

Epilogue

Naomi

Eleven months later

I did, in fact, lay an egg. It happened when I was about six months into the pregnancy. It was really weird, and pretty gross if I'm really honest. Although, I pretty sure human births get pretty gross too.

It happened exactly like the healer said it would. I started having cramps one day. It felt a lot like when you have a really brutal period. Before I knew it, I was pushing out a large, oval, gooey egg.

When I first started cramping, Octo went to get Xaiolpa. She rushed over and stayed with me the whole time. She was amazing. I was freaking out a lot, and she helped keep me calm.

Once the egg was out, we had to...attach it to our nest.

That part was—well—gross. There was a lot of goo in-volved. I prefer not to think about that part.

Once that was done, we just had to protect it and wait.

And we continue to wait. Having the baby still growing, but outside of me for so long is pretty unnerving. I've spent days just staring at the egg wondering how my baby is doing.

The egg is slightly translucent. We can see the shadow of the baby, but not enough to make out what he or she looks like.

Octo and I stay in our nest most of the time. The idea of leaving my baby so defenseless really scares me, so I haven't left much.

Octo goes out to get us food and do a really quick, shortened patrol of his territory. Then he comes straight back home. Vrala sent a couple of soldiers to help patrol Octo's territory while he's busy caring for me and our little one. So far, we haven't had any issues with humans and I'm pretty sure the soldiers are just bored all the time.

A while ago, Octo asked Vrala about the facility, but he dodged most of Octo's questions about it and wouldn't really tell us much. He did reassure us that he's personally keeping watch over it, and that we have nothing to worry about. I asked about that woman I saw, if he's seen her. He gruffly said he had, and wouldn't say anything else.

Recently Octo's gotten very growly and standoffish with males coming near our nest. He even acts like this with Ovaggd'tho, which surprised me. Xaiolpa explained that this is just how males of their species are when they have eggs that need protecting. Needless to say, it's been a while since we've been able to check in with Vrala or the soldiers. But Octo has assured me that they would still come to give us the news if there were things that we needed to know.

Cindy uses her scuba gear to come down and visit every day, and I love her visits. I can tell that she's already in love with the baby even though he or she is still in the egg.

Xaiolpa is also expecting babies. She's already laid three eggs, and now she's just waiting for them to hatch. She says she has about five months left to go.

We've gotten into the habit of taking turns visiting each other while our mates guard our little ones. It's been so nice to bond with her. She has become a second best friend to me.

Today is actually my day to visit her, but Octo and I noticed this morning that the baby is wiggling around in the egg a lot more than normal. Octo thinks it might be hatch day soon, maybe even today, so we're both staying in the nest.

We've spent the day curled up together with most of Octo's tentacles coiled around the base of the egg, holding it. The baby is getting more and more active as the day wears on, and now the egg is jerking around and moving a lot. Today has to be THE day.

I give Octo a nervous look. "Is there anything we should do to help?"

He continues watching the egg closely and shakes his head. "Don't worry, Naomi. Our baby will break out of the egg soon. I'm certain that they are strong and will fight their way out shortly."

Octo's right, because in the next hour or so, we see the egg begin to split. The split grows every time the baby pushes against it. Then suddenly the split turns into a hole and a little baby head pushes its way out.

"Oh, my gods!" I put my hands near the head, ready to catch the baby if needed. With one strong push, our baby wiggles out of the egg, and uses its tiny tentacles to swim into my arms.

On instinct, I immediately pull the baby to my breast to begin nursing.

I give Octo a wide-eyed look. He's looking at the baby with a mixture of awe and wonder.

"Octo...it's our baby!" My eyes fill with tears as I look down at our baby happily nursing on my breast.

He doesn't say anything, just gently strokes his palm on the baby's head.

"Octo, can you look—is it a boy or girl?" I ask.

Octo gently spreads out the baby's tentacles while the baby squirms and makes little grunting noises.

When he looks back at me, he has a huge grin on his face. "It's a girl." Then he looks down at her lovingly. "She's going to be so strong and powerful. Fierce just like her mother."

I smile at that.

I look back down at her and study her tiny features. She looks a lot like a human baby on her face and torso, except she's purple like Octo. When her tiny eyes open, I see that she has octopus pupils like Octo too. Her little tentacles are so adorable. They cling to me and wrap around my arm. She's absolutely perfect, and the most beautiful baby I've ever seen.

I lean back into Octo's chest as I cradle her to my breast. I look up at him and ask, "What do we name her?"

He looks thoughtful for a minute. "Do you have any names you like for a girl? We can give her a human name."

I shake my head. "It doesn't matter to me. Just something that I can say easily."

Octo chuckles. "How about Ziopi?"

I look down at my daughter. I'm not sure what kind of name she should have. I'm so unfamiliar with names from Octo's world. And I've never had any particular attachment to baby names in the human world either.

I pick up her little clawed hand and look at her tiny fingers. Trying the name out, I whisper, "Ziopi."

She opens her eyes and wiggles adorably.

I laugh. "I think she likes it." Then to her, I say, "What do you think, do you like Ziopi?"

She wiggles again, and I look back at Octo.

He smiles. "Ziopi it is then."

I relax back into his chest as he holds us safe in his tentacles.

As I look down at Ziopi, I say, "Thank you, Octo. Thank you for finding me and stealing me. It's been the best thing that's ever happened to me."

He runs his hand through my hair and says, "Thank you for staying with me, my mate."

The End

ACKNOWLEDGEMENTS

Thank you to everyone that loved Mushy Stuff and stuck around to take a chance on the second book in the Guardian Mates series.

Thank you to all of my beta readers for all the wonderful feedback. You helped me more than you can know.

Thank you to Lianne for another amazing cover, and for helping me with Octo's design. And for putting up with my endless back and forth of "let's make him hotter...no wait...let's go back to more monstrous!"

Thank you to my editor, Yarn Wyvern, for all the hard work, funny comments, and my horrible punctuation.

Thank you to my super supportive family for always believing in me.

When Lyra Lorne isn't daydreaming or writing, she can be found hiding from the heat in the sprawling suburbs of Texas. She enjoys spending time with her family and menagerie of pets and doing anything creative.

For sneak peeks into current projects and exclusive artwork visit www.lyralorne.com.